Nora S

bestselling author of *"the Coincidence of Callie and Kayden"*

ruin me

Jessica Sorensen

For information:

jessicasorensen.com

Cover Design and Photography: Mae I Design

www.maeidesign.com

Ruin Me (Nova, #5)

ISBN: 978-1503047556

Chapter One

Jax

Over the last few weeks, I've been having a dream about a girl I think I might be in love with; the taste of her lips, the softness of her skin as my hands travel all over her body, memorizing every inch of her. Even though the dream is fucking fantastic, I don't mind waking up. A couple of years ago, I would have. I wouldn't have been able to go to sleep in the first place.

Of course my new life has downfalls too. Like how I get woken up in the mornings.

"Ha, ha! Gotcha!" Mason laughs as he pours apple juice on my face.

My eyes shoot open, and I bolt upright in the bed as he runs out of the room, laughing. My hair and face are sticky and my sheet's a mess. The little rugrat. He's lucky I love him so damn much otherwise I'd be pissed.

"I'm going to get you back!" I shout at him, hearing fitful giggles bursting from the living room.

I wipe my face off with the top of my shirt then roll out of bed to take a shower. As I'm grabbing some clean clothes, my sister Avery sticks her head into my bedroom. Her brown hair is damp, and dark circles reside under her eyes.

She takes one look at me and sighs. "Aw, man, he got you, too."

"Yeah, and I'm guessing by your wet hair, he did the same thing to you." I select a pair of clean jeans and a grey shirt then slide the dresser drawer shut. "Apple juice?"

"No, mine was orange juice." She combs her fingers through her hair. Tiny flakes of pulp are stuck in the brown strands. "This gotcha game is getting out of hand. I wish Tristan would have never taught it to him."

"You should be glad he did. Tristan's a good guy. And, after everything you went through with Conner, you deserve good. You and Mason both do."

Conner is Avery's abusive ex-husband and Mason's father. After almost destroying their lives, he's now behind bars where he belongs.

She reclines against the doorframe with her arms folded. "I know he is, but I have to be honest; I'm a little bit nervous about him moving in."

"You'll be fine." I wind around the bed toward her. "You guys are good together."

"Yeah, we are." She stands up straight. "I just feel bad that you're moving out in a month."

"I'm not. As much as I've loved helping you out over the last couple of years, I'm ready to start my own life."

"I know. And you should be. But it doesn't mean we won't miss you any less." She sighs, her eyes welling up. Avery always gets this way when it comes to what she considers "me growing up too fast," even though I'm nineteen years old. But with a nonexistent father and a deadbeat, drug addict mother, Avery pretty much took on the role of my mother the day I was born.

"Come on. Come get a hug. You know you want one." I open my arms for her.

"You found a place to live, then?" Her voice is muffled against my chest as she hugs me.

"Yeah, you remember Clara McKiney, right?" I ask, and she bobs her head up and down. "Well, my place is in the same complex as hers."

"Is it in a good neighborhood?"

"It's in an affordable neighborhood."

"I don't want you living any place rough."

"It not rough. Just eccentric." Besides, with going to school full-time and my part-time job helping out at the college lab, it's all I can afford.

She moves back, dabbing her teary eyes with her fingertips. "Just promise me that, if you ever need any help at all, day or night, you'll call."

"All right, I promise." I draw an *X* across my chest. "But you do realize my place is only a ten minute drive from here. And you can stop by anytime." That seems to satisfy her, although I predict more waterworks in the future when I actually have to pack up and move out.

She makes a grossed-out face as she glances down at the orange juice soaking her shirt. "I'm going to go shower then make breakfast."

Avery is a terrible cook, yet always attempts to make nice meals.

I open my mouth to decline her breakfast offer, but snap my jaw shut when I realize there won't be many more breakfasts together for the three of us after I move out.

After I shower, I put on the ring my mother gave me when I was five years old. It's the only present I've ever received from her and honestly I think she forgot she gave it to me; otherwise she would have asked for it back by now. It's welded with silver and black and has a few diamonds in it. Girly, I know, but it belonged to my grandfather. At least, that's the story my mother told me. I wouldn't be surprised if she stole the ring while she was spun on crystal then conjured up a fairytale about where it came from.

I collect the car keys to the beat up Jeep I bought off Avery a month ago when she got herself a newer car. I'm heading to a party later tonight after I get off work. Lyle, one of my friends from Psychology class, is the one who invited me. I'm not much of a partier, because I usually spend a lot of time helping Avery with Mason. But after getting a better job and a more stable boyfriend, Avery's reached a groove in her life where she doesn't have to rely on me so much. Part of me is sad about the loss—I'd gotten used to being needed—but another part of me is relieved, like I can finally live my life without worrying about my sister or my nephew.

By the time I leave work, it's after eight o'clock at night. Fifteen minutes later, I arrive at Lyle's house, which is smack dab in the middle of the suburbs. The charcoal sky is smoldering with stars, and the muggy air is dense against my lungs and skin. But that's North Carolina for you.

"Hey, man." Lyle gives me a fist bump as I step into the foyer crammed with sweaty, drunk college kids, then he shoves a cup of beer in my hand. "You made it."

I scan the people's faces, searching for someone in particular—the person I came to this party for, the girl I was dreaming about this morning. "I told you I would." I sip the beer, despite not being a big drinker. I'm just really nervous about seeing Clara and need to chill out.

"If you're looking for Clara, she's in the kitchen." Lyle guzzles the rest of his beer and crunches the cup.

I take a swig of the frothy alcohol. "Am I that obvious?"

"Yeah…" Lyle's gaze tracks a chick wearing a tight red dress. "Hey… I'll see you later, okay?" He chases off after her like she's a magnet and he's made of metal.

I push my way through the mob and into the kitchen where I immediately spot Clara in the sea of bodies. She's near the counter by the booze, laughing at something her friend Dana is saying, her crystal blue eyes crinkling at the corners. She's holding a cup and must be a little bit drunk because she ends up spilling her drink on the floor.

"Whoops. I'm such a klutz." Her voice floats over the voices and music, swirling around me.

I linger in the doorway, watching her talk and laugh. I'm fixated on the way she keeps brushing her hair off her shoulder, the way her lips move, and how when she shifts her weight, the hem of her red and black dress curls against her long legs.

Finally, her friend spots me and leans in to whisper something to Clara. Clara twists around and her eyes find mine. She sucks her bottom lip between her teeth, and I know what she's thinking because it's the same thing that's on my mind.

I want to rip her clothes off. Take her upstairs and strip her bare. Kiss her and never come up for air again.

Okay, so her thoughts might not exactly match mine. At least the last part. Friends with benefits—that was the agreement we made three weeks ago after our third hook up. I have to remind myself it's all Clara wants. That she's not looking for more, even though I am.

She weaves around the people, pushing her way to me. "Hey, you." She grins as she reaches me. "How long have you been here?"

"Like ten minutes maybe." My heart does this stupid little pitter-patter inside my chest when her gaze deliberately drinks me in.

"I thought you were going to text me when you got here, so we could..." Her cheeks flush then she bites her lip again and looks away.

"Fuck," I finish for her, even though I'm a bundle of nerves.

I don't hate that I'm nervous. I prefer it. I started dating when I was sixteen, although the term "dating" might be a stretch since I never stayed with anyone for more than a few weeks. It wasn't like I bailed on the relationship. Things just crumbled the moment they realized I came from a shitty home and had a mother who whored herself out and was constantly doped up on heroin. I never took it too hard when they bailed out, because I couldn't really blame them.

When I was seventeen, I moved from my hometown in Wyoming to North Carolina to live with my sister. The list of reasons why I moved is endless. Shitty living environment. Crappy mother. My fifth stepfather had started using me as his punching bag. My mother had also disappeared at the time. Just up and left with no reason, something she did a lot. At that point, I didn't trust anyone. Hook-ups filled my weekends, and I never felt anything for anyone.

Then, a little over six months ago, I met Clara.

She was wearing scrubs with kittens on them the first time I met her, looking absolutely adorable. We quickly became friends. She made me smile. Laugh. She made me nervous in the best sort of way. One night, we accidentally hooked up at a party after too much Bacardi. Neither of us were drunk enough to forget what happened—how fucking amazing we were together. When the next weekend came, the same thing happened. I realized maybe I wanted to try the girlfriend and boyfriend thing. Problem is, Clara's still afraid of commitment for whatever reason, which is the main reason I haven't told her I'm moving into the same apartment complex as her—she's going to flip out.

She shakes her head, still avoiding eye contact with me. Her flush deepens. "You have such a dirty mouth."

"What? I'm just saying it like it is."

Our gazes weld, and her breath hitches in her throat.

"Fine, Jax Hensley, I thought you were going to text me when you got here so we could *fuck*." She elevates her brows, arrogantly challenging me, even though her face is bright red.

"Jesus, Clara." My eyes mockingly widen. "You're making me blush."

She swats my chest, laughing, and the sound is better than the music. "Ha, ha, you think you're so funny."

"No, I don't. I think I'm fucking hilarious."

She rolls her eyes. "All right, Mr. Hilarious. Where to this time?"

I chuckle lowly. "Always straight to the point."

"You knew that about me before we," she gestures between the two of us, "started doing this."

"True." I glance at the overly stuffy kitchen, the trashed living room, then at the narrow stairway leading upstairs. "Follow me, my lady." I offer her my hand, grinning.

She promptly shakes her head and shuffles back. In the beginning stages of our fling, I thought her offish behavior stemmed from her embarrassment to be seen with me, considering I'm a year and a half younger than her, but I know the real reason now.

I wait for her to say it.

Because she always does.

"No hand holding, remember?" she reminds me apologetically.

"Sorry, I forgot," I lie then push a path to the stairway that leads to the second floor.

I've only been to Lyle's house once so I don't know my way around. When we make it to the top of the stairway, I knock on the first door we come to. No one responds so I figure the room is vacant and open the door. I end up getting an eyeful of a couple ripping off each other's clothes. It would be fine—I mean it's not anything I haven't seen—except the dude's sporting an odd leather getup, which includes suspenders.

"Whoops." I slam the door then move to the next one.

"Be careful," Clara warns. "I don't want to see that again."

I rap my knuckles on the door. "What? Leather doesn't turn you on?"

"Not when it looks like that." Her face scrunches in disgust.

I laugh as I crack the door open and strain my ears for voices on the other side. After I'm convinced the room is vacant, I enter the small room and flip on the light.

"It's an office," Clara remarks, her gaze roving across the mahogany desk, bookshelves, filing cabinets, and leather chair.

"I can go check the other room." I turn around to leave, but she captures the hem of my shirt.

"No, this works." Her cheeks pink as she sucks her bottom lip between her teeth.

My brow arches. "You have an office fantasy or something?"

She reluctantly shrugs then releases my shirt. "Maybe." She gives me a sidelong glance and desire burns in her eyes.

"Busted." A grin curls at my lips. "You so do."

"So what if I do?" She faces me with her shoulders squared. "It's not that strange of a fantasy."

"Nope, not at all." I grin. "Do you want me to go find a suit and tie for you and put it on? I could dress the part of the powerful business man so you can play the naughty secretary."

"Whatever. You know me well enough that you'd have to play the naughty secretary and I'd play the dominant boss."

"All right, then." I span my arms out as I back further into the room. "Come on boss. Come dominate me." When my ass bumps against the edge of the desk, I hoist onto it with my legs dangling over the edge and wait. I fight back a smirk as she fidgets with the bottom of her dress, like she's unsure of what the hell to do next. "Oh, my God." I press my hand to my chest. "Did I actually strike Clara McKiney speechless?"

Her eyes narrow and she elevates her chin. "You know what? You asked for it." She struts toward me, emphasizing the sway of her hips.

My heart thumps inside my chest, like a goddamn drummer on crack. I grip the desk to stop from reaching out to grab her, wanting to let her do her thing.

"Aw, look at you and your swagger," I joke, my gaze drinking in the curves of her body.

"Jax?" She wets her lips with her tongue when she reaches me.

My eyes distractedly drop to her mouth. "Yeah...?"

"Shut up." She slams her lips against mine so forcefully our teeth clank together. I end up biting her lip, and she groans in response, grasping at the front of my shirt and yanking me closer. "Take off your pants," she breathes against my mouth then nips at my lip.

I willingly lean back, tug my shirt over my head, and discard it on the floor. Then our lips magnetize together, our tongues tangling as her breasts smash against my chest. She flattens her palm across my stomach and groans again, intensifying the kiss, sucking the breath from my lungs. My hands travel along her curves, grip her waist, and fist the fabric of her dress.

17

"Clara," I whisper huskily as my fingers travel to the bottom of her dress, "take it off."

She moves back, grabs the bottom, and lifts it over her head. Her eyes are wide and glossy as she chucks the dress on the floor, and her chest heaves as she stands vulnerably in her lacey bra and panties. I've never seen her without so many clothes on before. Usually she won't undress more than necessary.

Her skin is like silk, the curves of her body flawless, and I want nothing more than to bite her toned ass.

"God, you're beautiful." My hand drifts toward her, but her fingers enfold around my wrist.

"Slow." Her attention darts back and forth between the dress on the floor and me. She looks like she wants to get dressed again, but I kiss her before she can.

Gripping her ass, I pull her up on the desk. She whimpers as she lands on top of me then scrambles to try and climb off. I quickly cup the back of her head, tangle my fingers through her hair, and tug at the roots, guiding her mouth back to mine. I kiss her fiercely, and she relinquishes, straddling my lap.

My fingers sketch a path down her spine, causing a shiver to course through her body. Her back arches, and her hips thrust against mine as my hand reaches the bottom of her back. Even through my jeans, her warmth makes my cock hard. I moan as she lightly traces her teeth across my tongue. My body convulses as if I'm a fucking virgin again.

"Good fucking hell, this feels so good."

She pushes back, rakes her fingers through her hair, and then she stares down at me, her blue eyes sparkling like sapphires. "Take off your pants."

"You're really getting off on this bossy thing, aren't you?" I slip my hand underneath her ass to unzip my jeans.

She holds up her thumb and finger an inch apart. "Just a little."

"Fine by me." I wiggle my jeans and boxers down as far as I can get them with her sitting on me. Then my cock springs free, and she gasps from the contact.

I reach around her to unhook her bra, but she grasps my fingers before I can unfasten the clasp.

"I have to keep some boundaries," she says, struggling for air. "And I've already crossed a line with the dress."

I groan in frustration, but remember I agreed to this.

"Fine." I tuck my hands under my head and rest back. "Have your way with me then."

She angles her head to the side and her expression fills with uncertainty. "Do you… have something?"

"You know I do." My gaze remains fixed on her. "It's in my pocket."

"In the front pocket or the back?"

"The back." A lazy smile sprawls across my face.

She shakes her head. "You're so enjoying this, aren't you?"

"Enjoying what?" I ask innocently.

She playfully scowls at me. "The thought that I'm going to have to reach back there and feel your ass to get it."

"Now, why would I enjoy that?"

"I don't know. Maybe you like your ass getting fondled."

I glare at her and she grins wickedly. Then her hand dives underneath me, and she feels around until she finds the condom in my back pocket that I solely tucked in there because I knew this was going to happen tonight—it's becoming a Friday night routine.

She pinches my ass as she withdraws her fingers, making me flinch. "Don't pretend you didn't enjoy that." She smirks then tears open the wrapper with her teeth.

I don't deny it. I enjoy everything when it comes to being with Clara. I don't tell her that, though; otherwise she'll be out the door before I could even get my pants up.

She rolls the condom on my cock then moves her panties to the side and starts to lower herself onto me. Meeting her halfway, I raise my hips and thrust deep inside her. She gasps with her head tipped back and her chest arched out.

It's the goddamn sexiest thing I've ever seen.

Our hips grind together as we move rhythmically. Our skin dampens, and our breathing turns ragged. My body pleads for more.

"Jax," she cries out, her fingernails piercing my chest. "Harder."

She's usually a little more reserved during sex. Having been with only one other guy before I met her, she told me she was clueless in bed. It must be the role playing bringing it out of her.

Giving her what she wants, I grab her waist, grip her tightly, and pound her hard until she comes apart in my arms. My eyes close as my body gives one last jerk, and I push deep inside her.

I momentarily drift away from reality, wishing I could stay there forever.

When I open my eyes again, she's lying on top of me with her head tucked underneath my chin. My heart is pounding in my chest and I know she can feel it.

Knowing she'll only remain this way for a few seconds longer, I seize the opportunity to kiss the top of her forehead. "That was good," I whisper, drawing patterns on her back as I stare at the ceiling.

Moments later, Clara shifts off me to stand up. She bends over to scoop up her dress and slips back into it while I discard the condom and pull my jeans back up.

"So, now what do we do?" She bites on her thumbnail as she watches me pull my shirt over my head.

"We could do it again," I suggest as I stretch out my arms and legs.

She laughs like I'm joking, but I'm not. "No seriously." She checks the time on her watch. "I still have an hour before I have to go home. We could go get some ice cream or something. That is, as long as you're sober enough to drive."

At twenty-one years old, I find it odd that Clara has a curfew. Sometimes she tells me she has to go home early because of work, while other times she doesn't give a reason. Up until a month ago, I had to leave early too, because my sister Avery had been working night shifts and needed me to watch Mason. It makes me really curious what awaits Clara when she returns home.

While she rarely speaks of her home life, I know that she lives with her mother, and that her father passed away a couple of years ago. I've also heard funny stories about her quirky neighbors but that's about it.

"I had half a beer." I hop off the desk and ruffle my hair into place. "Sex and ice cream, huh? Sounds like a pretty good night."

"See, that's why I like you." She grins as she combs her fingers through her hair. "Anyone else wouldn't have wanted to leave the party to go get ice cream, but you totally get it."

"Get what exactly?"

"My ice cream fetish."

"Of course I do." I desperately want to hold her hand as we head for the door. The urge is so intense I have to ball up my hands to stop myself from touching her. "Just like I now get your bossy fetish."

"Yeah, thanks for helping me discover that one." She flashes me another heart-stopping grin as she reaches for the doorknob.

"I can't wait to explore more of your fetishes," I say a little too loudly while she's opening the door.

She shushes me, pointing a finger at me. "That's secret information right there, so be careful who you tell."

I drag my fingers across my lips. "You know my lips are sealed."

"Yeah, I know." Her posture relaxes. "Sorry if I've seemed a little bitchy lately. Things at home have just been intense."

"Want to talk about it?" I ask as we enter the packed hallway.

She swiftly shakes her head with her attention on the stairway. "No. I deal with it enough while I'm there, so why would I ever want to talk about it?"

"To let some steam off?" It's more of a question since I have no clue what the problem is. I wish I did, though. Wish she'd just open up to me.

Again, she shakes her head.

She remains quiet until we make it out of the house. Then we both let out a breath of relief as the silence and warm, humid night encompasses us.

"As hot as it is out here," she fans her hand in front of her face as she trots down the porch stairs, "it's like ten degrees cooler than the inside of that house."

"That's all part of the partying experience." I follow her off the porch, and then we hike up the driveway toward where my Jeep is parked.

"I've never been one for partying."

"Me neither."

"Because of your mom?" she wonders, staring at the road in front of the house.

I nod, my jaw tightening at the mention of my mother.

The gravel crunches under our shoes as we fall into an awkward silence. She makes a quick stop at a car so she can retrieve her phone and wallet.

When she closes the door, she sputters an apology, "I'm sorry. I know you hate talking about your mom out loud."

"It's okay." We reach the Jeep and I open the passenger door for her. "I never would have told you about her if I couldn't handle you bringing her up."

She looks remorseful as she swings around me. She must feel really terrible too, because she ends up giving me a quick kiss on the cheek.

"Thanks for tonight," she whispers then ducks in and closes the door.

A hint of a smile touches my lips as I round the back of the car. I hop in, rev up the engine, and then maneuver past the cars toward the road.

Clara retrieves her phone from her pocket. "I just need to text my ride and tell them I'm going home with someone else," she explains as her fingers hammer against the buttons.

"Dana?" I wonder as I drive toward the one ice cream parlor in town that's open this late.

She shakes her head. "No... Lyle gave me a ride here from work."

"Oh." I frown, feeling more jealous than I probably should. She's not mine. She can ride with whomever she wants.

"Don't be like that. Lyle and I are just friends." She reads me like an open book. "He had the same shift as me tonight and offered me a ride so I didn't have to take the bus."

"*We're* just friends." As soon as I say it, I wince, wanting to retract the words. "Sorry, can we just pretend I didn't say that?"

"As long as you'll stop being a weirdo about me getting a ride with Lyle. I don't think of him like that. I don't even find him attractive."

"But you find me attractive." I waggle my brows at her. "In fact, you find me so attractive that you're going to buy me cookie dough ice cream."

She sets her phone down on the dash. "How on earth does that prove I'm attracted to you?"

I shrug as I turn into the parking lot of the dimly lit ice cream store. "It doesn't, but I want you to buy me ice cream so I won't feel so cheap and used after the dirty stuff you did to me tonight." I flash her a lopsided grin as I park the car.

"After all the dirty stuff *I* did to you tonight?" She opens the door to get out. "Yeah, because you played no part in it."

I elevate my hands in front of me. "I was just lying there on the desk when you reached around and grabbed my ass."

"Jax," she hisses as a group of guys stroll by, "not so loud."

"Why? You shouldn't be embarrassed. Any guy would love for you to grab—"

She leans over the console and covers my mouth with her hand. The guys outside have stopped to listen, their attention causing Clara to boil with irritation. "You don't need to tell the whole world."

"Why? No one cares." My lips brush against her palm as I speak. "You don't know those guys over there, so what does it matter?" I don't want to fight with her. I only want her to say it, whatever it is that's stopping her from admitting she likes me.

"Because it does." An exhale eases from her lips then she lowers her hand from my mouth. "Now, can we please, pretty please, go get some ice cream? My treat. I'll even have them put extra cookie dough on yours."

I briefly consider refusing to get out of the car until she confesses her secret, but then a silent plea floods her eyes. It's the same look that got me into this situation to begin with—where I'm her friend/fuck buddy when really I want to be her friend turned lover.

"Fine," I surrender, opening the door. "But I'm only getting out for the extra cookie dough."

She smiles, then jumps out of the Jeep, and shuts the door. We cross the parking lot and stroll into the store. My phone starts vibrating as I'm scanning the menu, so I fish it out of my pocket. Tapping a few buttons, I open my texts while breathing in the sugary smelling air. Man, there's something about ice cream after sex that makes my mouth salivate.

Clara moves up to the counter to order while I check my texts. I quickly realize I have a new voicemail not a text. Strange, since I didn't even hear my phone ring.

The call was from an unknown number, but I don't think too much about it until I play the message and hear *her* voice.

"Hey, Jax, baby," my mother says in the high-pitched tone she uses whenever she's stoned. Even after not speaking to her for over two years, I still tense at the sound of her voice. "I was just calling to see how you were... see how stuff was going in North Carolina..." I hear rustling in the background then the bang of a door shutting.

"Okay, look." Her voice rings with panic. "I need you to come home. I've gotten myself into a bit of trouble with the wrong people and if I don't give them money, things are going to end badly. Jax, please pick up the phone. I know I've been a really shitty mother, but I'm still your mother and I—" Shouting cuts her off. "Jax help me. Marcus is going to k—." It's the last thing she says before the line goes dead.

I move the phone away from my ear and gape at the screen. Even with all the messes my mother has gotten herself into over the years, I've never heard her that worried. I don't want to care about what's going on, but I find my mind racing with different scenarios. All centered around one main thought, based on the last thing she said. She didn't fully get out what she was going to say, but my mind fills in the blanks.

Marcus is going to kill me.

Chapter Two

Jax

For the next several seconds, time passes by in slow motion. I have no clue who Marcus is, but my bet is he's a drug dealer my mom pissed off, maybe enough to kill her.

As Clara's paying for the ice cream, I manage to snap out of my trance and dial back the number my mother made the call from. My pulse quickens when the operator announces the line has been disconnected.

"What the hell?" I mutter, checking the time and date of the missed call.

Yesterday morning. God dammit! I really need to stop ignoring my phone so much.

"Is everything okay?" Clara asks as she hands me a heaping cup of cookie dough ice cream. "You look like you've seen a ghost."

I distractedly take the ice cream from her, still clutching my phone. "Heard from one is more like it."

Her gaze falls to my phone. "Who was it?"

I look from my phone to the ice cream then at her. Her expression carries compassion, her lips are slightly swollen from our kissing, and her hair is tangled from me running my fingers through the strands. I want to focus on her and forget about the call. Want to live in the present, not the past. But my mother's fearful voice is making it difficult to think about anything else.

Jax, help me.

"It was my mom," the words slip from my lips.

Clara's eyes pop wide. "Your *mom* was just on the phone? The mom you haven't spoken to since you moved here?"

"Well, it was only a voicemail, but yeah." Not knowing what else to do, I shovel a spoonful of ice cream into my mouth.

Clara absentmindedly stirs her ice cream as she studies me. "What did she want?"

The cashier is eavesdropping on the conversation as he refills the sprinkles, so I take Clara by the elbow and steer her toward the door. Once we're outside, I let go of her and jerk my fingers through my hair.

"She said she needed help. That she's in trouble with some guy named Marcus. That he's going to kill her. Then the line went dead." I blow out a stressed breath. "I know I shouldn't be worried—she doesn't deserve my worry—but I am."

"Jax, she's your mom, and you're a good person, so of course you're going to worry." She pauses. "Do you care if I listen to the message? Or is that too personal?"

I easily hand over the phone. I trust her, despite the fact that she doesn't trust me yet. She puts the phone up to her ear, and her skin pales as she listens to the message.

"I think you should call the cops," she says as she hands me back the phone.

"And tell them what?" I start across the parking lot toward my car. "I'm not even sure what happened exactly. I tried to call my mom back but the line's been disconnected. That's normal, though. When I was growing up, I hardly ever had phone service because she'd spend the bill money on drugs."

"Couldn't you call someone back home to go check on her?"

"I don't talk to anyone back at home anymore."

"You could always file a missing person's report. Then the police at least have to go look at the house, especially if someone is after her." She stuffs a spoonful of gooey ice cream into her mouth.

"I doubt they'll check on her, even with the voicemail." I pat my pockets for my keys then open the door for Clara. "Not just because she's an adult and there's a certain amount of time she has to be missing, but because the police are way too aware that she pulls this kind of shit all the time."

My mother has made it habit of vanishing over the years. Avery and I used to file reports when she was missing for more than a few days, but when I reached the age of about sixteen, I realized it was pointless. The police had stopped putting effort into finding a woman who had countless misdemeanors, including drug possession, prostitution, and assault. Besides, she always came back eventually.

She'll come back again.

She always does.

But she sounded so scared. My mother rarely sounds terrified since she can't usually feel fear through the heavy amount of drugs in her system.

"I have an aunt that lives in the same town," I tell Clara as she slides into the torn leather seat of the Jeep. "I haven't talked to her in forever and she absolutely hates my mother, but maybe I could call her and convince her to go check on things."

"I still think you should call the police first and see if they'll do it." She straps the seatbelt over her shoulder. "After that message, it'd be better for the police to check up on her."

I sigh heavily. I've already falsely reported her missing over a dozen times. Worried or not, the idea of calling the police is embarrassing. Still, after hearing her message, I'd be a shitty son if I didn't. "Fine, I'll give it a try."

"Do it as soon as you can." Clara smoothes her thumb between my brows, erasing the worry lines. "So you don't have to worry." Her eyes widen at the awareness of her intimate gesture and she hastily withdraws her hand. "I should get home. It's getting late."

Nodding, I close the door.

We make the short drive to her house eating our ice cream and listening to Coldplay, and don't really speak much until we're pulling up to the two-story apartment complex she lives in.

Like every other night when I drop her off, her muscles wind into knots when she reaches for the door to get out.

"Thanks for tonight." Even though the cab is dark, I can feel her blushing. "I had fun."

"Anytime." I force a light tone, despite the worry jostling around inside me.

"Call me if you need anything." She pushes open the door, then swings her feet to the curb and slides out. She starts to shut the door, but pauses. "You know what? Call me tomorrow and let me know what happens. I want to know you're okay." She closes the door and hurries up the sidewalk toward the entrance doors of the complex.

Elation swells inside my chest, but it quickly deflates as I start the drive to my house, wondering what to do about my mother. What if she's already dead? Do I really care? Guilt forms a big, old, air-restricting lump in my throat. Whether I love or hate my mother, I still need to find out what happened to her.

As soon as I make it home, I call the police department. I use the house phone so I can play the officer the message. He tells me they'll check up on it, but only out of obligation.

"Jax, you know she does this stuff all the time," Officer Del Monterlis sounds really annoyed, as if my phone call has ruined his entire night.

"I know, but I need you to at least swing by her place and check up on her. She said she was in trouble with Marcus. And it sounded like she said he was going to kill her before she got cut off."

"We don't know that for sure."

I sink down onto the mattress. "What else would the k stand for?"

He sighs into the receiver. "Fine, I'll stop by and see if I can find any signs of foul play, but I'll put money on it that the message you got was simply over the fact that she was under the influence. She's been arrested for drug possession and driving under the influence three times over the past two months. In fact, she might have left you the message so she could stage her disappearance and avoid her trial."

Sadly, he could be right.

"As for this Marcus guy," he continues, "he has a rep for dealing, but that's about it, so I'm guessing, if he did threaten her, it was an empty threat. You know how those things go when someone's living that type of lifestyle."

"Yeah, I know." I thank him for his help, and then we hang up with the promise of him calling me back. I decide not to tell Avery until I hear back from him. There's no

37

point in getting her all riled up if this turns out to be nothing.

By the time I lie down to go to bed, it's after two
o'clock in the morning. I fall asleep quickly but sleep like
shit for most of the night, tossing and turning and constantly waking up.

When my phone rings at sunrise, I'm already up and
dressed. I answer it, crossing my fingers it's Del and he'll
have good news.

"We didn't find her," Del immediately tells me after I
say hello. "And, other than the door being busted in, the
house is about as trashed as it was the last time I was over
there."

"Why was the door busted in?" I sit down on the edge
of the bed and stare out the window. The sun is shining in
the clear sky, and the trees are green with leaves. So bright
and cheery, yet I feel so dark inside. "That has to be suspi-
cious, right?"

"Normally, yes, but when it comes to your mother, not
really. Every time we get a call from her, the house is
trashed in one way or another, usually from the people she
lets into her home."

"But what if that's not the reason this time? What if
she really is in trouble?"

"There's still not much we can do. She's an adult who has a habit of disappearing when she needs to."

I massage my temples as pressure builds under my skull. "I know, but I just have this feeling that something's wrong."

"Something's always wrong when it comes to her, Jax," he replies exhaustedly. "There's a huge file on my desk right now of the missing reports you and Avery have filed over the years."

"I still think I should fill out a new one," I tell him. "Just in case."

He sighs then drones on about the details of the procedure. Twenty-four hours after I first called, I can fill one out, but there's not a whole lot they can do because she's an adult. I can tell he doesn't believe anything happened to her and that he doesn't he care. I want to be angry with him, but really, his attitude is justifiable. My mother has pulled a lot of shit over the years, gotten into a lot of trouble, pissed off a lot of people. Drugs have hardened her, and she's not a good person. Not even a little bit.

I hang up, feeling more unsettled and frustrated than I did last night. I drag my fingers down my face. "Fuck. What am I going to do?"

Even though I don't want to, I call my Aunt Julie, my mother's older sister and the one relative I have contact information for. She won't be thrilled to hear from me—she never is.

When she doesn't answer, I leave an awkward message, telling her who I am and asking her to call me back. Then I leave my room to get some breakfast and wake up Avery so I can explain what's going on.

Usually, Avery and Mason sleep in late on Saturday mornings, so I'm surprised when I enter the kitchen and find her in front of the stove, cooking breakfast. Pans are sizzling on the burners, and the counters are covered with eggshells, sticky yolk, and melted butter. My jaw drops at the sight because the air isn't smoky, the fire alarms aren't going off, and all hell isn't breaking lose.

"Good morning," she says without looking at me.

"Wow, that actually smells good." I breathe in the scent of bacon and eggs. "It's a miracle."

At the sound of my sullen voice, she whips around and almost drops the fork in her hand. "What's wrong?"

"Who says anything's wrong?" I feign ignorance.

"Don't play dumb with me." She aims the fork at me, a glob of grease dripping off it and onto the floor. "You're using your depressed voice."

"Yeah, I know." I take a seat on a stool and decide to just rip off the band-aid. "It's Mom."

Avery grinds her teeth, "What'd she do now?"

Not knowing any better way to explain it, I turn on the speakerphone and play the voicemail message.

"I called the police to go check on her," I explain after the message ends. "They said the door was busted in, but other than that, there's no sign of foul play. They said we could file a missing person's report in twenty-four hours, but I can tell they're not going to do anything."

"Do you really blame them? She's brought this on herself." She fumbles to turn off the burners, so flustered she practically rips off the nobs, and I start to regret telling her. "Who's Marcus?"

I shrug. "Your guess is as good as mine."

"Probably her pimp," Avery mutters. "Or her drug dealer."

"I called Aunt Julie." I get up and start cleaning the counters with a dishrag to distract myself.

"Really?" Avery raises her brows. "Why? She hates Mom. And she's never really been a fan of us since we're our mother's offspring and share the same DNA."

I lift my shoulder and give a half shrug. "It's the only thing I could think of to do."

"What'd she say?" She removes a pan from the burner and the grease stops sizzling.

I grab the trash bin from under the sink and wipe the eggshells into it. "She didn't answer, so I left a voice message."

Avery opens her mouth to say something, but seals her lips shut when my phone rings.

Grabbing it off the counter, I check the screen. "It's Aunt Julie," I say then press talk. "Hello."

"Hey, Jax. You called?" Julie asks, sounding about as annoyed as Avery did when I told her the news of our mother.

There's an uncomfortable pause as I rack my brain for what to say to her.

"You don't have to explain," my Aunt Julie says before I can speak. "I already know about your mother."

"How?"

"Because she called me a couple of mornings ago and told me she was going to call you after I refused to help her get out of the mess she's in."

My head slumps forward. "Who is it this time?"

"I'm not sure… She didn't say." She blows out a loud breath. "But Jax, I'm not going to lie to you. It sounded bad."

I pinch the bridge of my nose. "How bad exactly?"

"Bad enough that I wouldn't be surprised if her body turned up in a ditch somewhere," she says bluntly.

That's the one thing I remember about my aunt. Back when I was younger, and she still tolerated my mother's lifestyle enough to visit us, she would always say things how they were. *"Your house looks like shit. You look strung out. You need to take care of your kids better."*

"Maybe I should come home…" I trail off as Avery shoots me a dirty look. "Just for a week to see if I can figure out what's going on." I hope by saying this, she'll offer to do it herself.

"Well, I wouldn't if I were you. I'm sure as hell not going to waste my time looking for her," she replies bitterly. "She's not worth the hassle."

"Yeah, I guess not." I frown. Guess I'm back to square one.

The rest of the conversation centers on lighter subjects—how I'm doing, how Avery and Mason are doing.

She ends the phone call quickly, telling me to stay in touch, but I can tell she doesn't really mean it.

"You're not going home by yourself," Avery tells me sternly as I shove my phone into my pocket.

"You could always come with me," I suggest as I grab the broom from the pantry.

"I can't do that." She sets the fork she's holding down on the counter. "I'm not ready to see her or that house again."

"Neither am I," I mutter as I sweep up the eggshells on the floor. "But I think I have to."

"Why?" she gripes. "You don't owe her anything, and I don't know why you feel like you do."

"I don't feel like I do... it's just..." I don't know how to explain how I feel.

When I left my mother two years ago, it was for good reasons. But in the back of my mind, I knew she wouldn't be able to take care of herself. It's not like she could while I was living there, but I'd been old enough when I bailed out that I could stop her boyfriends and pimps from beating her. Help keep track of the bills. Help her keep her head above the water. Part of me knew, when I'd walked away, there was a possibility that she would wind up dead in a ditch somewhere.

"Look." I prop the broom against the wall, round the kitchen island, and place my hands on Avery's shoulders. "I know it might seem crazy, but I just need to go back and check on things. See for myself."

Avery shakes her head, aggravated. "What about school and work?"

"My last class was Thursday and I'm sure I can take off work for a week. I haven't used any of my sick days or vacation time yet."

Her gaze flicks to the fork, like she's contemplating jabbing me in the eye with it so I can't make the thousand some odd miles drive back home. "Only a week? Then you'll come back home?"

I nod. "One week is all I need to spend searching for her."

She sticks out her pinkie. "Swear on it. Swear you'll come home after a week even if you can't find her." I reach out to hook my pinkie with hers, but she pulls back. "And you won't go alone."

"I don't want to make you come with me."

"I'm not going to. I already told you I'm not ready to go back there." She glances at the hallway. "Take Tristan with you. He's from there."

"As much as I like Tristan, I don't know him well enough to do that." I restlessly thrum my fingers on the sides of my legs.

Who could I take with me? Who knows about my mother enough that it wouldn't be awkward? A thought strikes me straight in the skull. One I like, but have no clue how to make happen.

"I have an idea," I say then hitch my pinkie with Avery's.

Her brows furrow. "Who?"

"Clara." I smile for the first time since I got the call. Going home is going to suck balls, but if Clara goes with me, it might not be so bad.

"The nurse?" Avery asks, confused.

"Technically she's a CNA, but she's going to school to become a nurse."

With our pinkies still locked, she considers my solution. "You think she'd go with you? Are you guys that close?"

I waver at her question. Although I've told Clara a lot of stuff about me, there's still things I don't know about her. "Sort of. I mean, she knows about Mom and everything."

I have zero confidence that Clara will easily agree to make a road trip across the country with me, but perhaps with a bit of persuading, I can convince her. I just need to make her an offer she can't refuse.

Besides, even though I'm still not positive my mother is actually dead, it'll be nice to have someone I care about with me in case that's where this journey ends. Even if that person won't admit she cares about me, too.

Chapter Three

Clara

I'm having that dream again, the one about the car accident.

My father is lying in the street, surrounded by bent pieces of metal and shards of glass. My mother is still stuck in the car, and the passenger side door so crunched in, I can't get it open. The vehicle that side swiped us is several feet away, smashed into a streetlight post. People are gathering around, crying, calling nine-one-one, while I stand in the middle of the madness, unscathed except for a cut on my head and a stabbing pain in my arm.

"Daddy," I whisper as I inch toward him. The glass crunches under my shoes and the air smells like burnt rubber. "Dad…" I trail off at the sight of him.

His eyes are open and his breathing is wheezy. There's so much blood on the ground and around him. At first, I just stand there, staring helplessly at the scene. But then my father whispers my name and I snap out of my trance.

Kneeling beside him, I slip off my jacket to use to put pressure on the hole in his stomach, which seems to be the main cause of the bleeding. I take his hand and try not to cry. Try to be strong.

"Everything's going to be okay," I lie. Deep down, I know the truth—this is bad and more than likely will end in tragedy.

"Where's... your... mother...?" My father gasps, and his eyes are unfocused as if he's drifting off to a place only he can see.

Hot tears bubble from my eyes and spill down my cheeks. "She's fine," I lie, knowing it might be the last thing I ever say to him.

"Good." He almost smiles. "Take care of her, okay?" His head slumps to the side and silence surrounds us.

"Dad," I sob as tears pour from my eyes. "Daddy, please don't leave me."

Silence.

"Dad... please."

My blood roars in my eardrums.

A rooster crows from somewhere.

Roosters crowing...?

Huh?

My eyelids spring open and a feather lands on my forehead.

"What the hell?" I bolt upright in bed and pluck the purple and teal feather from my head. I spin the feather around between my fingertips. "Where on earth did this thing come from?"

As if responding to my question, a rooster crows from somewhere nearby… from somewhere inside the apartment. Throwing the covers back, I plant my feet on the carpet and pad over to my partially opened bedroom door.

My skin is damp from the dream I was having. Well, not really a dream. More of a memory of that day three years ago when I lost my father. It's been so long since I dreamt about that day that I forgot how exhausting remembering could be.

Sighing, I step out into the hallway to find out why I heard crowing. I instantly stumble back as a rooster flaps its wings, and feathers spew through the air.

"Mom!" I cry then flinch as the rooster pecks at dust particles and its talons claw at the carpet. "Could you come here for a minute?"

The rooster crows again then barrels toward me, looking as evil as the devil himself. I skitter around the bird and it ends up diving into my room. I slam the door, locking the crazy bird inside, then scramble down the hallway to the living room.

My mom is camped in the recliner in front of the television, laughing at what appears to be a soap opera. Even though I cleaned yesterday morning, the place is a mess—wrappers on the floor along with empty soda cans, clothes piled on the couch. There's also a trail of feathers leading from the front door to the hallway.

"Mom, why's there a rooster in the house?" I should sound more shocked, but sadly, these sorts of things happen all the time in the McKiney home.

She shovels a handful of popcorn from a bowl on her lap. "It looked sad, so I thought I'd bring it home."

I sigh, less surprised than I was to begin with.

Not only did the car accident claim my father's life, it left my mother with several injuries along with a few bolts loose in her head. It's not like she's insane; she just gets confused easily and does strange things like haul evil roosters home because they look sad.

"Mom, we can't have a rooster in the apartment." I start picking up the wrappers and throwing them into the trash bin.

"But it doesn't have a home. I feel bad for it." Her eyes remain glued to the TV screen as she stuffs her mouth with popcorn. She spends a lot of her days this way—watching reruns and soaps, and rarely leaving the apartment.

"Where did you even find a rooster?"

It's not like we live in farmland. We reside in a small town in North Carolina, close enough to the beach that you can usually smell salt in the air. The weather consists of humidity, humidity, and more humidity, sun, and the occasional rainstorm.

"Mr. Garlifed had it." She aims the remote at the television and flips through the channels. "He kicked it out, though. Said the thing was watching him while he slept."

The apartment we've lived in for the last three years isn't located in the best neighborhood. The affordable area tends to draw in unique characters, like Mr. Garlifed who likes to constantly monitor the people coming and going from this place and who apparently owned a rooster. But with my mother unable to work because of her disabilities and me being the sole provider, it's the only place I can afford. Hopefully, after I graduate with my nursing degree, I'll be able to change that. But, since I have to manage my time between school, my job, and taking care of my mother, graduating is still a long ways away.

The rooster crows again as I'm scooping up a pile of clothes to take to the laundry room. "It can't stay here, Mom. I'm going to have to give it back to Mr. Garlifed and have him take care of it."

"But what if he kicks it out again?"

"Then he kicks it out."

"I want to keep it," she whines. "I need the company."

"You have Nelli and me as company."

Nelli is my mother's sister and my aunt who damn near saved my life. She came around a lot after the accident, helped out whenever she could. When she retired, she offered to start sitting for my mother while I went to school and work. She doesn't charge me anything, says she's happy to do it.

"But I want someone who's here all the time," my mother gripes. "I want a pet."

"We'll find you something better than a rooster," I tell her then hurry down the hallway toward the laundry room.

After dumping the clothes on top of the washing machine, I grab a broom and prepare to open the door and chase the rooster out of the house. It's times like these when I wish my older sister, Lizzy, didn't live clear across the country. I think about it every day. How much I wish she were here to help take care of our mother. How much less stressful my life would be. But my sister has her own life in Seattle with her husband and two children.

"I just can't do it, Clara," she said the day after our father's funeral. "There's just not any room in our place, and I have Jenna and Kessington to take care of. My plate is already too full. You don't have anything except your job and school."

"But we don't have a place to live," I told her, terrified of facing the future alone. "I can't afford the house Mom and Dad were living in."

"Maybe you can buy your own place with the money I'm sure they left us in Dad's will." She took my hand and gave me that look, the one she always gave when she had made up her mind about something. "And if all else fails, you could always put her in a home." Then she kissed my cheek and left for her hotel.

The next morning, she flew back home to her family. She has called me about ten times total over the last three years, because calling me is, "too painful of a reminder of everything she lost."

And the money is my father's will? Nonexistent. Turns out, my parents hadn't owned anything. My father's store had been run off loans. Most everything went back to the bank and I was left to start over. The problem was, at the time I was only eighteen-years-old, and I had no clue what I wanted to do with my life. I didn't have a job, at least not one that wasn't seasonal work. I had enrolled in college and was planning on just having a general major until I could figure out what I wanted to do. The plan was to take a year or two, try out some classes, see what piqued my interest.

That entire plan vanished in the blink of an eye, and I had to make big decisions quickly. I found us a place to live and dropped my enrollment to part time, so I could find a better job. I was hired as a temporary secretary at the hospital and enjoyed the environment so much that I decided I wanted to work there permanently. I trained to become a CNA, which is my current job. Three months after changing careers, I switched my major to nursing.

Even though I've managed to take care of us, I still have those moments. The ones where I want to break down and consider putting my mother into a home. Those thoughts make me feel guilty. The last thing my father asked me to do was take care of her. What kind of daughter would I be if I just bailed out? Besides, my mother can't help how she is.

She used to be a brilliant professor at the local college I now attend part time. She taught Sociology and Psychology. She used to play this game where we'd sit in a public place, and she'd give a mental analysis of people passing by. I sometimes wonder if inside her own head, she's assessing her own brain, if she knows she's broken and is trying to figure out why.

I jerk from my thoughts and wrap my fingers around the doorknob, preparing to enter the rooster zone. With a deep breath, I pull open the door.

As the rooster comes racing out with its beady little eyes locked on me, I wave the broom at it, careful not to hit it, and shoo the bird toward the front door. I knock a lamp over in the process, and the rooster punctures a hole in the leather sofa that I found in a second hand store for dirt cheap.

After a minute or two of doing circles around the room, I manage to get the damn evil bastard out the door.

"Holy shit. Roosters are nuts." Panting, I turn to my oblivious mother who hasn't even looked up from the television through all the commotion. It makes me want to cry. Everything does these days.

"That was so funny." My mother chuckles, munching on popcorn.

I count backwards to ten before moving away from the door. Then I give my mother a quick kiss near the scar that runs from her temple to the back of her head, remnants of the accident. "I'm going to go get ready for class. Nelli should be here soon. Can you please, please let her in when she gets here?"

"Sure honey." She finally looks up at me for the first time this morning. Sometimes I find it painful to look at her, because she looks the same as she used to, except for her eyes. They carry a void, as if she can't quite figure out who I am or where she is. "Don't forget to scatter your father's ashes like he wanted. At the Tetons."

She says this to me every day, even though I don't have the time or money to drive across the country to do so. My father made the request in his will: *I want my remains scattered from one of my favorite places—the Teton Mountains in Wyoming.* I feel terrible that I can't, and tried to talk my sister into doing it a few times. But she always refuses, saying she doesn't have time.

After I leave the living room, I pick out a pair of jeans and a T-shirt, and then duck into the bathroom to take a shower. Afterward, I get dressed, run a comb through my lengthy dark brown hair, apply a dab of liner and lip-gloss, and tug on my favorite pair of boots.

I exit the bathroom with a trail of steam following me. I collect my bag and books from my bed then head for the front door to go to my last class of the semester.

My mother and Nelli are huddled together in the living room, laughing about something. They're only a few years apart, with graying hair, and similar facial features. The biggest difference between their looks is the scar on my mother's head and the fact that my mom wears a lot of bright colored clothes, one of the few traits that stuck with her after the accident. As always, my mother looks happy. She always does when Nelli's around.

"Hey Clarabell Tellamell," Nelli says when she notices me lingering in the doorway.

She already has tea and cookies set out on the coffee table, along with a book. Nelli spends a lot of time reading my mother's favorite novels to her.

"Hey, Nelli Bellie full of Jelly." I make up a nickname to use back. It's a game we play sometimes—see who can come up with the best rhyming names. "Just a quick note. She might try to convince you it's okay, but do not, under any circumstances, let a rooster into this house."

"Yes ma'am." Nelli salutes me. "Now stop worrying and get going before you're late to class." She focuses back on my mother. "What do you think? Tea or the book first?" Her voice is gentle and my mother warms to it.

Nelli's gentleness makes it easy to leave the house without me feeling as though I'm abandoning my mother.

"Clara, wait!" my mother calls out.

I turn around. "Yeah?"

She motions for me to come over. "I need to talk to you."

I walk over. "What's up?"

She gestures for me to lean closer then whispers, "Don't forget to scatter your father's ashes. We're running out of time." She presses a small piece of paper into my palm.

I look down at what she gave me—a photo of lofty, snow-covered mountains pointing toward a crystal blue sky.

"Who took this picture, Mom?" I smooth my thumb along the creased photo. *So this is where my father wants to be laid to rest. It's pretty.*

She simply smiles at me. "It's pretty, isn't it? Your father sure loved it there. And, if you don't get his ashes there soon, it'll be too late."

"Too late for what?"

"For him to get his peace."

I tuck the photo into the back pocket of my jeans then turn to Nelli. "Make sure she takes her pills this afternoon,"

59

I tell her. "She's been spitting them out a lot lately, at least when I give them to her."

"Would you stop worrying and get going?" Nelli flicks her wrists, shooing me toward the door. "I've been taking care of your mother long enough to know the routine."

I hitch the handle of my bag over my shoulder. "Sorry. The rooster thing must have stressed me out or something."

I wave goodbye to the both of them, crack the front door open, and stick my head out. After I check for the rooster in the poorly lit hallway, I step out and cautiously walk past the numbered doors, heading toward the exit. When I make it outside without crossing paths with the crazy bird, I breathe in relief.

The sun blares down on me as I start up the sidewalk and veer toward the bus stop on the corner of the street. But I slam to a halt when a Jeep Wrangler pulls up to the curb in front of the complex. I try not to grin as Jax Hensley leans over and opens the passenger door. Grinning will only make this thing between us more complicated, make our arrangement mean more than it is. And the last thing I need in my life is another side-blinding complication.

Jax is a year and a half younger than me, although you would never guess it. Not only is he extremely responsible—one of the things that drew me to him—but he looks older too. With brown hair, hazel eyes surrounded by dark eyelashes, and full lips that I always find myself biting whenever we're making out, he drips adorable sexiness.

"What are you doing here?" I approach the vehicle but don't get in. I haven't heard from him since the night he got a call from his mom. He'd sent me a text, telling me stuff went okay. He was pretty vague, but I didn't have time to analyze it since I worked the nightshift on Saturday. "I thought we only met up on Fridays."

"I know, but I want to pick up some stuff from the store and knew it was your last class today, so I thought, what the hell. I might as well pick her up." He dazzles me with a charming grin, the same grin that got me into this whole mess to begin with.

The day I met him, I was a hot mess—late for class, wearing my scrubs with no makeup on. I smelled like someone who hadn't taken a shower in four days and looked like I was riding on only three hours of sleep, which was exactly what had happened.

As I was sprinting to make it to class on time, I'd sprinted around the corner of the building and slammed into Jax. My books flew everywhere, and I just about started to cry due to exhaustion.

I clumsily bent over to grab my books and he crouched down to help me.

"Hey, I know you, right?" he asked as he handed me my Chemistry book.

I glanced up to a pair of hazel eyes studying me so intensely that I wanted to hunker down and hide.

"I don't think so." I grabbed the book from him and hurried down the hallway to class.

He followed me.

"What are you doing?" I hugged the book to my chest as I rushed passed people with him striding along right beside me.

"Going to class." He seemed amused and not at all bothered by my attire. In fact, I caught him checking me out once or twice. "That is what people generally do at college."

I stopped in front of the door of my English class, and he halted with me.

"But you're not in this class," I pointed out.

"Aren't I?" he quipped. "Funny, I thought I was."

When I gaped at him, he laughed, this full belly, crinkling-around-the-corner-of-the eyes laugh. It was probably the most beautiful sound I'd heard in a long time. Such freedom to his laughter and I envied him because of it.

62

"I usually sit in the back, so you probably haven't noticed me." He stuck out his hand. "I'm Jax Hensley."

I shook his offered hand. "Clara McKiney."

"It's nice to meet you, Clara McKiney." He gave my outfit a once over. "Cute scrubs, by the way." His lips twitched with amusement then he swung around me and walked into class.

It seemed like I should have been insulted—scrubs aren't cute and I looked like crap—but for some reason, I felt flattered enough to smile. After that, I started noticing Jax a lot. We quickly became friends and stayed that way for about six months.

We were tipsy the first time we fooled around, but not enough to blame what happened on the alcohol. I told myself the next morning it was a one-time thing, but then the next weekend came. We were at a party, laughing and drinking. Then we were suddenly sneaking back to one of the bedrooms and ripping off each other's clothes. The third time happened in the backseat of his Jeep, parked out in the parking lot of my apartment. I'd realized that night that, if this thing between Jax and I was going to keep occurring, it had to be a strict friends with benefits type of arrangement because I don't have time for a relationship.

Plus, my life's too complicated. He'd agreed to my terms, and thus began Friday nights filled with sweaty, hot sex.

"Car rides to class aren't supposed to be part of the arrangement," I say, but scamper into the passenger seat when I hear a piercing crow from nearby.

"Why? I used to give you rides all the time before," he reminds me as I close the door.

"I know. Sorry I'm being a pain in the ass again. I just had an… interesting morning." I toss my bag into the backseat, buckle up, and discreetly check him out. Today he's wearing a fitted black shirt that shows off his lean muscles I crave to touch.

"You know, we could make our weekend start now," he says when he notices me admiring him. "I could pick you up after class and we could go back to my place."

I turn my head toward the window to hide the first grin that's graced my lips since Friday. "Can't. I already have a hot date today."

"You're such a liar." His tone is playful, but also carries an edge.

Deciding not to toy with him this morning, I meet his gaze again. "Alright, I'll play nice today, but you owe me."

His smile conveys all kinds of naughtiness. "Oh, I plan to pay you back in full."

My skin tingles with excitement at the things he'll do to me, things he's done to me, the way I've let him touch me.

I've only been with one other guy before, and that was in high school, so hooking up with Jax has been a very new, interesting experience for me. One that I'm enjoying and want to keep enjoying. As long as we follow the rules, things should work out fine.

"You're blushing, Clara," he teases, brushing his finger across my cheekbone.

"I'm not blushing," I lie then roll down the window, letting in the humid May air. "It's just hot in here."

"Whatever you say." His lips quirk.

I roll my eyes, but then flinch when I hear the cry of a deranged rooster.

"Is that…" Jax peers over his shoulder out the back window. "Do I hear a rooster?"

I sigh. "Yeah, I think our neighbor has one."

He turns his head back to me with his brow arched. "Here?" He skims the two-story, indoor complex with zero lawn space. "Really?"

"Yeah, remember my crazy neighbor I told you about? The one who keeps a log of the visitors that come through the apartment?"

He nods. "What? Is he keeping chickens now?"

"Roosters." I cup my hand around my ear. "Chickens don't make that God awful noise." I lower my hand to my lap. "And not only does he keep roosters, but he also kicks them out because they watch him sleep, and then my mother takes pity on them and brings home."

"Your mother let a rooster into your place?" he asks.

I instantly realize how crazy that must sound, since Jax doesn't know about my mother's condition.

"She's one of those people who loves animals." Which is kind of true. Before the accident we had two cats, a dog, and one very obnoxious bird that repeatedly chirped, 'I'm so sexy.'

Jax balls a fist over his mouth, his shoulders shaking as he fights to restrain his laughter.

"You can laugh. Now that it's all over, it's pretty funny. Although, if you'd asked me ten minutes ago when the crazy bird was in my room, and I'd have told you it was possessed." I tap my finger against my lip. "Hmmm… Maybe Mr. Garlifed was on to something. Maybe it was watching him in his sleep. Those beady eyes did look a bit shifty."

"Or maybe he's into voodoo," he jokes along with me. One of the things that drew me to Jax is his ability to not only tolerate my odd sense of humor but he can make jokes with me too.

My lips part in mock shock. "Oh, my God. I think you might be onto something. This entire time, all the logging he's been doing was actually to keep track of all the people he put curses on with his pet chickens."

"Roosters." He cranks the wheel and pulls the Jeep forward onto the road while giving me a wink. "Jesus Clara, get it right."

"I'm so sorry." I melodramatically press my hand to my chest, glad I didn't fight the ride. Like always, whenever I'm around Jax, I feel way more like my old self. The Clara who freely bounced through life, made jokes whenever she could, and didn't have to worry about the bills piling up on the kitchen counter. "But, to be fair, you did kind of make the incorrect reference first."

"I blame that on my nephew." He steers the car up the main street lined with quaint stores that sell items like beachwear, seashell wind chimes, and homemade baskets. "He's always confusing animals."

"How is Mason doing?" I prop my boots up on the dash and relax back in the seat.

"He's doing well. Getting bigger and smarter by the day," he says as he turns toward a small drive-thru coffee shop located about a mile from the college. "You should come over sometime and see him."

"Maybe one day." I force a stiff smile, feeling like an asshole for lying. The truth is, I'll never go over to Jax's house. He lives with his sister and nephew and going there means meeting his family. And meeting his family feels way too personal for friends who mess around on the weekends.

Jax knows me too well and sighs, reading through my bullshit. "So, do you work tonight?" he asks as he pulls up to the order menu.

"Not until Wednesday." I lean over the console to scan the list of beverages. This close to him, I catch a whiff of his cologne and a hint of cigarette smoke. "I thought you quit smoking."

"I did, but I messed up this morning."

"Why?"

He shrugs. "Just one of those days."

I'm about to press for more, worried something might be wrong, but he speaks first.

"I don't know why you look at the menu," he teases. "You always get the same thing."

"Hey, maybe I'm planning on mixing it up," I retort, swatting his arm. "Perhaps I've decided to become adventurous today and live life on the wild side."

He glances at me as the lady through the intercom asks what she can get him. We're so close our lips almost brush, but he doesn't lean away. He elevates his brows, challenging me. "Alright, Miss Adventurous, what'll you have?"

I think about kissing him, planting a big, wet kiss right on his mouth. Three years ago I would have. Three years ago I was Miss Adventurous.

But not anymore. I've become Miss Routine.

I end up ordering a Vanilla Cappuccino with an extra shot, just like I always do. When I lean back in my seat, Jax looks mildly disappointed, but doesn't comment. Instead, he traces a finger down the brim of my nose.

"So, what's on the agenda for this weekend?"

"Well, I can only go out for about two hours," I tell him as he pulls up to the window. "I have work and stuff."

He mulls something over as he hands the cashier a ten. "What other stuff?"

"Just stuff." Mom stuff, like doctor appointments and making sure she's taken care of.

"Could you maybe get some time off from work? I want to spend a little more time with you this weekend."

"More time to do what? I mean we only need like two hours for us to," I gesture between the two of us and shimmy my hips, "make bow-chicka-bow-wow."

He chuckles under his breath. "You know, the really amusing thing is that you make the joke and make yourself blush." He grazes his finger along the corner of my eye, causing me to shiver. "But I don't just want to make bow-chicka-bow-wow this weekend."

My brows knit. "What else would we do?" School's out, so studying isn't an option. Back in the day when we were just friends, we used to go to movies and dinner but now I worry it'd end up being a date.

"I was thinking we could take a road trip," he mutters then coughs into his hand.

"What?" I figure I heard him wrong. I had to have heard him wrong.

He clears his throat. "I want you to take a road trip with me."

"*Now.*"

"Well, after your last class gets out today." He reaches out the window, takes the coffees from the cashier, and then he hands me the cup marked cappuccino.

"Jax, I can't do that." I swallow a drink of the coffee but instantly regret it as the steamy liquid scalds my tongue.

"You can't say no yet." He places his coffee into the cup holder. "Not when you haven't heard where we're going and why."

"I don't need to hear why. I can't go."

"Why not?"

"Work…" I start to list things off, but realize, with school ending, the only other responsibility I have is my mother. And while it's a huge responsibility, Jax doesn't know about it.

"You have a ton of vacation time, right?" He shoves the shifter into first gear and drives forward.

"I'm saving that up for a family vacation," I lie, feeling like a class A jerk. But telling Jax about my mother means letting him enter the madness of my world.

"To scatter your father's ashes with your mom? In the Teton's, right?" When I nod, a faint smile touches his lips.

"Well, what if I said, during our road trip, we'd be right by the Tetons?"

I scrunch up my nose. Crap. Why did I ever give him that information about my father?

"Your mother could even come too if she wants," he says, though he sounds unenthusiastic about the idea.

"Why are you even going on a road trip right now?" I ask as I put the coffee between my legs and flip down the visor to block out the blinding sunlight.

His jaw tightens as he merges the car onto the road. "It's my mom."

"I thought you said she was okay?"

"No, I said everything was okay, meaning I have a plan."

"You omitted the truth." I rummage around in my bag for my sunglasses.

"I did it for a reason." The gears grind as he shifts into second gear.

"What reason?" I find my sunglasses and slip them on.

"Because I needed time to come up with a plan to convince you to come with me."

"On a two thousand mile road trip to Wyoming?" My eyes are wide and my jaw is hanging open. He has to be joking. Then again, I've been noticing lately that he's started seeking more in our relationship.

He cracks his knuckles against the steering wheel then grazes his thumb over a black and silver, diamond-studded ring he sometimes wears. "Look, I know what you're thinking, but before you start listing all the reasons why you can't go just hear me out." He pauses, giving me a chance to protest. Even though I want to, the plea in his tone keeps my lips fastened. "I need to go back and at least try to find my mom. The cops aren't going to do anything—no one will—and I really need you there with me. Just as friends. In case I lose my shit or something... because, being back there," he swallows hard, "it's going to be hard."

Jax has told me enough about his past that I understand. But going with him on this trip feels dangerously intimate.

"I get where you're coming from. I really do. I couldn't imagine not knowing where my mother was..." I bite on my fingernails. "But I don't think I should be the one to go with you. Avery would be a way better choice."

"Avery isn't ready to go back there." His grip tightens around the shifter, his knuckles whitening. "Honestly, I'm not sure I am, either."

"Isn't there anyone else who can go check up on your mom? Like your aunt?"

"I called her the morning after I got the voicemail. She doesn't want anything to do with this." He slows down the Jeep to turn into the parking lot of the college, then parks near the front and pushes the shifter into neutral, leaving the engine idling. "I know this is a lot, but I wouldn't ask if I didn't need your help. And the Teton's are really close to my hometown. We could swing up there and scatter your father's ashes."

A lump wells in my throat at the idea of standing with Jax on the mountain as I say a final goodbye to my father. The real kicker is how easy I can envision him there with me. But then what? After it's all over, we'd return here, and I'd have to go back to my hectic life.

"Please don't ask me to do this," I whisper, grasping the door handle.

He swallows hard at the crack in my voice. "Okay, yeah. You're right. I shouldn't pressure you like this." His smile is fake and his eyes radiate pain.

I don't relax at all as I open the door and hop out of the car. I start to shut the door, but pause. "Are you still going?"

He sucks in a gradual breath while staring at the trees in front of the car. The sunlight reflects in his hazel eyes and highlights the pain in them. "I have to; otherwise, I'll never stop worrying about her."

"Are you leaving right now?"

He nods, his gaze gliding to mine. He looks so vulnerable that I just want to hug him. "I'm heading home to pack, and then I'm hitting the road."

"You're going to take someone else with you, though, right?" The idea of him doing this alone makes me want to cry.

"Sure." He's lying.

I want to help him, but instead I close the door and watch him drive away, picturing him all alone in that car heading to a place that's always caused him pain.

As the car vanishes out of sight, the image of him shifts to me at eighteen years old, handling funeral arrangements by myself. Taking my mother to doctor appointments. Handling the will. Bills. How my life crumbled. How I lost most of my friends. How my boyfriend broke up with me, said my life was too complicated for him.

"I don't think I can do this anymore, Clara," Mack told me two weeks after the funeral, right when bills and responsibilities had really started to pile up. "Our lives are too different now. You're always so busy and you have a ton of responsibilities."

"I'll make time for you." I felt like I was being strangled, as if the last piece of my world was about to be ripped out from underneath me.

He scratched uncomfortably at the back of his neck. "I don't know. I just don't see this working out. All those plans that we had to travel are gone. Well, for you anyway... I can still go."

Looking back at that moment, I'd felt such hatred for him. But at the time, I couldn't process my feelings because I was too terrified of being alone. I had just lost my father. My mother was only mentally half there. My sister had bailed out. I had no one.

"But I thought you loved me?" It was what he told me when I lost my virginity to him: 'Clara, I love you, so, so much.' Maybe I'd been naïve to believe him.

"I'm sorry," he said with a shrug.

Tears had stung in my eyes and I loathed myself for being so weak. After just watching my dad die, the pain of a breakup should have seemed insignificant. But all I kept

76

thinking was: *alone, alone, alone.* "I know I've been kind of distant lately, but I just need some time to get stuff together."

"Clara, this isn't a problem that's just going to go away." He looked at me with pity. "If I stayed with you, it'd mostly be because I felt sorry for you. We'd eventually end up ruining each other."

"Please, don't leave me... If you love me you'll stay," I pathetically begged, clutching onto him.

He gave me a kiss on the cheek and his lips achingly burned my skin. "I'll see you around okay." Then he walked away, leaving me alone with responsibilities I wasn't ready for, but had to deal with.

I didn't have time to fall apart, to mend a broken heart, so I vowed to go on alone. Vowed to never trust anyone that much again.

Even though my legs desperately beg to chase after Jax, I listen to my heart and walk away.

Chapter Four

Clara

Jax haunts my thoughts all through the final exam. I think about him when I'm gathering my stuff and heading off campus. On the bus ride home. By the time I walk into the living room of my apartment, I have a Jax worry-induced headache.

I decide to send him a text to check up on him, hoping it might alleviate some of my anxiety.

Me: U doing okay?

Jax: Yeah.

Me: U hit the road yet?

Jax: Heading out of the driveway now. C u in a week :)

I feel even worse and the smiley face at the end of his message makes me feel like a gigantic asshole.

After I put my phone away, I drop my bag onto the sofa. My mother and Nelli are in the kitchen baking brownies.

Or Nelli is baking and my mother is licking the batter off the spoon.

"How was your day?" Nelli asks as I trudge into the small, narrow kitchen.

"Fine." I open the fridge and grab a can of soda.

"Oh no. That doesn't sound good," she replies as she butters the pan.

"What do you mean?" I pop the tab on the can. "I said it was fine."

"In the most depressing tone I've ever heard." She picks up the bowl to dump the batter into the pan.

"What's wrong?" my mother asks, for a fleeting moment appearing like her old, concerned self. But then she drops the spoon onto the floor and doesn't bother picking it up as she hoists herself onto the countertop.

"It's nothing." When Nelli shoots me a stern look, I sigh. "One of my friends wants me to go on a road trip with him to his hometown in Wyoming so he can check up on his mother. She has a lot of problems with drugs and has gone missing. He wants me to come with him and I feel really bad because I can't."

Nelli scrapes the batter from the side of the bowl. "Why can't you go?"

I give a discreet glance in my mother's direction. "Because I have other responsibilities."

Nelli sets the bowl down, picks the baking pan up, and opens the oven. "I can watch her for you, Clara Bear." She slides the pan into the stove, closes the door, and then sets the timer. "That's what I'm here for."

"That's not your responsibility."

"It's as much mine as it is yours."

"No, it's not. I'm her daughter."

She wipes off her hands with a dishtowel. "Honey, why do you think I'm here all the time?"

I shrug. "Because you're my mom's sister."

"That's true, but that's not the only reason I come over." She glances at my mother then leans in and lowers her voice a notch. "Before any of this happened, I made a promise to your parents that, if anything happened to them, I'd take care of you."

I vaguely recollect reading in the will that Nelli had guardianship if something happened to my parents before my sister and I turned eighteen.

"But I'm not a kid anymore," I utter quietly. "I don't need to be taken care of."

"Yes, you do." She pinches my cheek like she did when I was a child. "You're only twenty-one. You're life's just getting started."

"This is my responsibility. I've been doing it for three years... Dad asked me to."

"Honey, we've been over this a thousand times. Your father may have asked you to take care of your mom, but it doesn't mean he wanted you to sacrifice your happiness to do it."

"I'm happy."

"No you're not."

Deep down, I know she's right. But it's difficult to admit aloud.

"I'm not telling you that you have to stop taking care of your mother," Nelli says. "You can still keep doing it when you get back, but you also need to take a break sometimes. Get out and live a little." When I remain reluctant, she adds, "Unless that's not the only reason you don't want to go."

"I have work too," I feed her a lame excuse.

She never buys my bullshit. "I'm sure you have vacation days saved up since you never take time off."

I have every intention of lying to her. But she gives me a similar look to the one my mother used to give me whenever I was lying, and I end up caving.

"The person who asked me too go on the road trip is a guy I have a very complicated relationship with."

Her brows elevate as she opens a cupboard to put the sugar away. "How complicated?"

My Aunt Nelli may be cool, but I'm not about to tell her about Jax and me being fuck buddies. "Just normal complicated."

She acutely eyes me over. "All relationships are. That's just part of life."

I restlessly tap my foot against the floor. "I'm not ready to get close to someone. And, even if I wanted to, I don't have the time. Being in a car with him for that long… something will happen between us. I know it will."

She sets the spoon and bowl into the sink and then flips the faucet on to rinse them off. "If that's all it's going to take for something to happen between the two of you then my guess is that it'll happen whether you go on the trip or not."

I frown. She's saying my worst fears aloud.

"I'm not telling you that you have to go." She unties the tie on the apron and hangs it on the handle of a drawer.

"But I think you should. You could use a break. You never smile anymore. You used to smile so much. I miss my Little Sunshine Girl."

So do I.

"And you could scatter your father's ashes while you're there." My mother lowers her feet to the floor as she stands up. "Wyoming is right where the Tetons are." She's fully aware of reality at the moment, something that happens occasionally, and it's almost too painful to witness, because we know at any moment she's going to slip away from us again.

"Mom, don't you want to be there when I do that?" I ask as she crosses the limited kitchen space. "To say goodbye."

"I already said my goodbye at his funeral. Besides, you know I can't be in a car for that long. Not after the accident." She places her hand on my cheek and a smile reaches her eyes. My heart squeezes in my chest at the brief glimpse of my mom, the one before the accident. "Your father would want his baby girl to do it. You were always his favorite." She runs her hand over the top of my head, a gesture she used to do when I was younger when she tucked me in at night. "Be his happy girl again instead of looking so sad all the time." Moments later, my mother vanishes inside herself again. "Time to watch my favorite show." Her eyes light up and she practically dances to the recliner.

My heart cracks, and I massage my aching chest. "I'm not sad all the time. Why does everyone keep saying that?"

Nelli gives me a sympathetic pat on the shoulder. "Go call your work then pack your bags," she says then joins my mother in the living room.

I collect my bag from the sofa then go to my bedroom. My frown etches deeper as I enter the room barely big enough for my bed and dresser. Feathers are all over the carpet and my comforter. I pick up a trash bin near the foot of the bed and start picking them up with a timer ticking backwards in my mind. Jax said he was leaving when I texted him, which means I only have about ten minutes before he's out of town and on the road. I've already killed at least five minutes in the kitchen. I'm running out of time.

But you shouldn't even be thinking about going, anyway.

My thoughts bounce back and forth like an out-of-control bouncy ball. Right and wrong. Fear and want. Heartbreak and happiness. God, if my father could see me now, he'd be so disappointed. He used to call me his Little Spitfire, a seize the day, blue-eyed girl. He said he envied my sense of adventure.

I remember the day he gave me the nickname. I was eight-years-old and we'd gone on a family vacation to an amusement park. There was this one monstrous rollercoaster that rose to the sky and dropped to the ground that my mother and sister refused to go on. Me, I bound right up to the ride with my father hurrying after me. We rode it together, screaming our lungs off. Only when we got off did I admit to my father that I'd been terrified of riding it.

"Then why'd you get on it so easily?" he wondered as we walked toward the exit.

I shrugged. "Just because it looked scary, doesn't mean it didn't look fun. Besides, if I didn't go, I'd be standing around with mom and Lizzy and that just seemed super boring."

He smiled down at me and took my hand. "You know what my Little Spitfire, I envy your sense of adventure. I really do."

My eyelids shut and lift as I blink from the memory.

"This thing with Jax… it doesn't have to mean more than what it is," I whisper to myself as I stare at my reflection in the mirror. Like my mother, I look pretty much the same as I did before the accident, though dark circles permanently reside under my eyes now. "You can just go as his friend and be there for him. You don't even have to have sex with him. Things could just be like they used to."

Before I can talk myself out of it again, I pick up my phone and dial Jax's number. He answers after three rings.

"Hey… what's up?" He sounds stressed out.

I summon a deep breath. "Turn back around and come get me. I'm going with you."

"Are you sure?" I can almost hear the smile in his voice and a grin emerges on my own lips.

"Yep, I'm positive," I reply, hoping I'm not making a mistake.

Hoping when the trip is over, Jax and I will still be… well, whatever we are.

Chapter Five

Jax

Clara has barely uttered two words to me since I picked her up from her apartment five hours ago. She packed pretty light—one small suitcase, her purse, and a black vase that carries her father's ashes—and hopped into the car looking terrified out of her Goddamn mind.

I tried to chat with her during the beginning of the drive, asked her if she got time off from work. She replied with a simple, "Yes." I asked her if there was anywhere specific she wanted to stop. She uttered, "The Tetons." I asked her if she was going to be okay scattering her father's ashes without her mom. "I have to," was her only response. Then her hands clenched into fists, and her eyes welled up, so I quickly dropped the subject and concentrated on the road while Clara fixed her attention on my iPod.

After about six hours on the freeway, I pull off an exit ramp to get gas. It's late, the stars are twinkling in the clear summer sky, and the florescent lighting of the gas station flows into the cab of the Jeep as I park in front of the pump.

"I'm going to go to the bathroom," Clara mutters as she nudges the door open with her elbow. "You want me to get you anything?"

I shake my head, even though I'm starving. But I feel like shit. Not only because I'm heading home, but because I can tell Clara doesn't want to be here with me.

She hesitates then heads inside the gas station while I climb out of the Jeep, scan my card, then recline against the pump as I wait for the tank to fill up.

Through the store window, I spot Clara when she exits the bathroom. She veers to the right and over to the soda section. Her lips are moving, and she keeps tugging her hand through her hair as if she's freaking out. She does this movement where she raises her hands in front of her, like she's chewing out the air, then she shakes her head, lowers her hands, and yanks open the cooler door. After snatching up a few sodas, she makes her way down an aisle and to the register.

The cashier is a guy in his mid-twenties with a beard and hair to his shoulders. He flashes Clara a few smiles, says something and then laughs. He's probably flirting with her. I don't blame him. Even in frayed shorts and a faded tank top, she's sexy as hell.

When she walks out of the store, my suspicions are confirmed as the cashier leans over the counter and checks out her ass. He watches her all the way to the Jeep then notices me noticing him and hastily looks at the register.

"Hey." Clara smiles as she strolls up to me with a bag full of goodies in her hand.

"Hey?" I reply more as a question, her sudden cheery attitude throwing me off.

She offers me another smile then gets in the car, right as the gas pump clicks. I remove the nozzle and collect my receipt before sliding into the driver's seat.

Clara retrieves a bottle of Dr. Pepper from the bag and places it into the cup-holder. "I got you two of these because I know they're your favorite." She digs around in the bag. "And a bag of Cheetos, M&Ms, and mints." She grins proudly. "I think I got all your favorites."

"Yeah... you did," I turn the engine while studying her. "Did you do a line of crack in the bathroom or something?"

"No, I was planning on saving that for the motel room," she jokes. "Why?"

"Because you seem a lot happier than you did five minutes ago. I mean, you've barely said two words to me the last four hundred miles."

"I know." Sighing, she leans over the console to put the bag of snacks on the backseat. "I've been a super crappy road trip buddy so far, which is really sucky of me. Don't worry, though. I gave myself a pep talk while I was in the store, so I'm back in the game."

"Is that what your weird little hand thingy was? Because it looked like you were chewing out the coolers."

She scratches the back of her neck. "I probably should have done it while I was in the bathroom. I think the cashier thought I was nuts."

"I doubt that." I flip on the headlights. "He was checking out your ass while you were walking out."

"Can you really blame him? I have a great ass."

"Yes, you do," I agree as I drive onto the road and head toward the onramp, glad to have my Clara back.

She grins as she tears open a bag of Skittles, but then her expression turns serious. "Jax, I'm really sorry for being a downer. I just felt a little guilty for leaving my mom at home."

"Why? Because she gets lonely?" I subtly press for information, hoping I can figure out what on earth goes on at her home.

"Kind of…" She shakes her head. "Can we forget I said anything?"

I try to read her, but she lowers her chin and allows her hair to fall forward to block her face.

"Okay, sure." I focus on the road. It's late enough that the highway is pretty desolate, peaceful, quiet, which makes the drive relaxing.

"So, how far are we going to go before we pull over and sleep?" Clara asks as she turns on "Can't Forget You" by My Darkest Days. She places the iPod back into the stand on the dash then slips her flip-flops off and rests back in the seat. "Or are we just going to do rotation and cruise the whole way through?"

"That really all depends."

"On what?"

"On how well of a night driver you are." Holding onto the steering wheel with one hand, I pick up the soda and fumble to twist the lid off. "I can go for a while, but I'm not going to be able to stay awake the entire way."

Clara must get tired of watching me struggle because she snatches the bottle from my hand and unscrews the cap before returning it. "Truthfully, I'm not the best. I actually have to wear glasses when I drive at night."

"Really? I don't ever remember you wearing glasses." I take a drink of the soda then set the bottle back in the holder.

"That's because I try not to drive at night solely because of that."

"I bet you look cute in them." I gather her hair in my hand and pile it up on top of her head. "Like a naughty librarian. Maybe we could do a recap of Friday night when we pull over. Only this time, you can pretend to be a naughty librarian."

"And what would you be?"

I shrug. "A guy who wants to do a naughty librarian."

She snorts a laugh, but then her shoulders slouch. "Actually, I've been meaning to bring up our arrangement to you." She scratches at the corner of her eye as she stares at the green glow of the stereo. "I think we should set some new ground rules for this trip."

"More rules?" I pout. "We already have a lot."

She stares at my jutted out lip then nibbles her own. "I know but," her gaze collides with mine, "it just seems like doing anything while we're spending this much time together could end up being a disaster. Besides, it's not Friday."

"Yeah, but there'll be a Friday in," I look at the clock on the dashboard—nine-fourteen, "less than four days."

"Jax," she begs with her hands clasped in front of her, "please, please, pretty please don't make things complicated."

My pout deepens, but I surrender. I owe her that much for coming on this trip with me. "Fine, but only on two conditions. One, you don't judge me based on anything you see during this trip."

"I would never, ever judge you," she says, shocked. "Besides, I already know how bad your mom is."

"Yeah, but you haven't seen the shithole I grew up in."

"I'm sure it can't be any worse than where I live now."

I think about telling her right then that I'm moving into the same apartment complex as her. She couldn't run away from me, either, not until we got home. But it seems like a dickhead move when she's driving clear across the country with me.

"Just promise me." I reach for my drink again.

"All right, I swear."

"And two, you play a road game with me."

"What kind of a road game?"

"How about the game of pull over the car and give me road head?" I suggest with an innocent shrug.

Her eyelids lower as she pinches my side. "Watch it, buddy. You're breaking my new rule."

I chuckle, rubbing the spot she pinched. "What? You said we couldn't fool around, but perverted jokes are fair game. Besides, we'd get bored if we didn't banter."

She doesn't argue. "We could play I Spy."

"Or twenty questions."

"No way. That game is too dangerous."

"Why? What are you hiding Clara McKiney?"

"Nothing." She averts her gaze to the backseat. "Hey, I forgot I bought gum."

"Saved by the subject change," I tease her as I reach for the iPod and skip to the next song. "How about if we play truth, but promise to keep the conversations light?"

She sits back in her seat with a stick of gum in her hand. "It still sounds kind of dangerous."

I wiggle my brows at her. "Where's your wild side?"

She unwraps the gum and pops it into her mouth. "I haven't seen her in like three years," she mutters. Her gaze travels to the back of the Jeep where the black vase is seat belted in, just in case we hit a bump or something. She suddenly squares her shoulders. "All right, lets play truth. But let's make it a lightning round. Make things interesting." Her voice quivers as if she's scaring herself.

"Are you sure?" I check. "Because we don't even have to play a game if you don't want to."

"Favorite color?" she starts the game without missing a beat.

"Blue, but you already knew that." I hurriedly think of a question. "Favorite food?"

"Pizza." She points a finger at me. "You knew that already, too."

"There's too much pressure doing a lightning round," I say at the same time she sputters, "Favorite sexual position?" She pulls a whoops face as she slaps her hand across her mouth.

"The Standing Wheelbarrow," I answer with a grin. "I can't believe you asked that question. You have such a dirty mind."

"That was an accidental question," she protests, lowering her hand to her lap. "And I've never heard of the position. I think you're making it up."

"It's not made up. And I'll prove it to you one day." I smirk when she fakes a scowl. "What's your favorite position?"

She fidgets with a hem of her shorts. "I don't know... um, doggie style."

"Have you ever even done that position before?" I ask with an impish grin.

She shoves my shoulder, causing a slight swerve of the steering wheel. "Oh, shut up. You know I'm limited on my knowledge, but that doesn't mean I'm an idiot."

"Hey, easy, you're going to make me crash." I steady the wheel as I laugh. "So, have you?"

"It's not your turn to ask a question," she says, grinning. "Favorite car?"

"A 1969 GTO Judge," I answer easily. "Now, have you ever done doggie style before?"

She huffs an irritated breath. "You're relentless."

"Yeah, so. Answer the question."

She shakes her head. "No, I haven't, okay."

"Don't worry, we can try that position one day, too." I wink at her, trying to lighten the mood.

She rolls her eyes, but I notice she squeezes her legs together like she's totally getting turned on. "Favorite dessert?"

"You covered in chocolate."

She massages her temples with her fingers. "This game is already getting out of hand."

"You're the one who suggested doing a lightning round. I'm just doing what I'm supposed to and saying the first thing that pops into my head. I can't help it if all of my thoughts are dirty." I pause, giving her a chance to say something. When she doesn't, I continue with my next question. "Favorite song?"

She props her feet up on the dash. "That question has, like, a hundred answers."

I drum my fingers on top of the wheel to the beat of the song flowing from the radio. "Okay, favorite instrument, then?"

"Um, I don't know. I can't play anything but I really like the sound of the violin." She briefly considers her next question. "Why do you always wear that ring?"

"That's a pretty random question."

"I'm just wondering why you wear it a lot. It looks kind of... feminine." She bites her lip, looking guilty. "Sorry, that probably sounded rude."

"No, it's fine." I graze my thumbnail across a diamond on the band. "It's the only present my mother's ever given me. She said it was my grandfather's who I've never met, but I'm not quite sure how true that story is. If it is his, though, then he had pretty girly taste." I can tell she feels sorry for me. Not wanting a pity party, I ask my next question. "Favorite eye color?"

"That's really your next question?"

"It's a very important question."

"Okay, green." She rolls her tongue in her mouth to keep from laughing.

"Ouch, that one hurt." I mock being offended.

"All right, I was lying. It's actually hazel."

"Go figure. My eyes are hazel."

"*Really?*" Her jaw falls open, and she pretends to be shocked. "I've never noticed."

"Ouch again." I press my hand to my chest, pretending to be deeply wounded.

She laughs, throwing her head back, and it's one of the most beautiful sights I've ever seen.

"Favorite trip?" she asks after her laughter silences.

"This one."

"This can't be your—"

I cut her off. "This is the only one I've been on besides when I drove out here. And I was covered with bruises and had a broken arm then, so the trip pretty much sucked."

She swallows hard. "Why did you have bruises and a broken arm?"

I shrug indifferently. I didn't mean to say it aloud and ruin our fun. Damn speed game. I don't have time to think before I speak. "I got into a fight with one of my stepfather's."

She stammers, "I-I'm sorry… I never knew things were that bad for you."

"It's not a big deal. The past is the past." I lopsidedly smile. "And now I get to be on the same trip with you, so everything turned out okay in my opinion. Well, as okay as the situation can be."

The air grows heavy, yet there's a charge to it, a buzz that comes before lightning.

"Everything's going to be okay." Clara places a hand on my knee, her fingers trembling the slightest bit.

"I hope so," I reply thickly. "I'm not positive that it's going to be, though. But at least I'll know what happened to her and won't have to spend my nights creating crazy what if scenarios."

"If this does end… badly, just know I'll be here for you," she continues, giving my knee a gentle squeeze. "I may suck at a lot of stuff, but I'm a pro when it comes to coping with the hard stuff."

I search her eyes, noting they're starting to water up. "Like with your dad?"

"And other stuff…" She withdraws her hand and faces forward again. "Look, there's a lot of stuff you don't know about me that hardly anyone knows about me."

"I already knew that."

"How?"

"I can just tell sometimes." When she frowns, I add, "Don't worry. I'm not going to ask you what your secrets are. Just know that I'm here for you if you ever feel like you need to tell someone and get some stuff off your chest."

She bobs her head up and down, staring out the window. "Thank you. You're a good friend."

There's that word again, the anti-Christ of my life. *Friend.*

I'm just crossing my fingers that, by the end of the trip, things might change. That maybe, just maybe, Clara will finally open up to me, and we can move forward in our relationship.

Chapter Six

Clara

At around four o'clock in the morning, we stop in a town in Indiana and get a motel room. I took over driving around three o'clock, so I'm sporting my glasses. On top of that, my hair is in a messy bun, my clothes are wrinkled, and the stench of junk food oozes from my pores. Jax is seeing me at my worst right now. Thankfully, he's already seen me like this quite a few times so it doesn't bother me.

"I so need a shower," I announce as we walk into the motel room.

Jax peeks inside a doorway to our right. "Well, you're in luck. There's a shower-bathtub combo in there that looks semi-decent. That is, if you don't mind dark rings around the tub."

I make a gagging noise. "I think I'll keep my flip-flops on the entire time."

We had to go cheap since Jax doesn't have a ton of money. I offered to chip in even though I can't afford to, and was relieved when he gave me an are-you-kidding-me look.

The room has the basics: a queen bed, a nightstand, and a television. The air is musty and dirt stains the carpet, but it works for me.

"I feel like this is an adventure." I drop my bag onto the floor, fling the curtain open, and peer out at the view of the freeway. "Slumming it in cheap motels, cruising on road trips. All that's left to do is hit up a rave, and I'll be able to check off all the things I missed out on when I was graduating."

He chuckles as he tosses his duffel bag onto the bed. "Is that what you think kids do when they graduate?"

Shrugging, I turn toward him. "Don't they?"

He unzips his bag. "Not really." When I frown disappointedly, he adds, "We can pretend, though."

"Sounds good to me. Guess we'll have to find a rave to hit up," I say, my voice dripping with sarcasm.

"I'll put it on the list," he replies, equally as sarcastic.

"Can't wait." I crouch down in front of my bag and grab a pair of boxer shorts and a tank top along with my toiletry bag. "Shower time for me."

"Want some company?"

I give him a blank stare. "Really?"

He retaliates with an aren't-I-so-innocent look. "What? I had to try."

I shake my head and let strands of my hair fall forward to obscure my smile. I can feel Jax's eyes following me as I cross the room and slip into the bathroom. I lock the door, hoping it will help my bubbling nerves of having to share a bed with him.

I give myself a pep talk while looking at my reflection in the mirror. "This is ridiculous, Clara, you're a grown woman. You can sleep with a guy and be just fine."

The terrified expression on my face does nothing to help my anxiety. Jax has been making me smile left and right during this trip, so much so my mouth actually aches. Nelli's Little Sunshine Girl is surfacing in full form. The problem is that I'm eventually going to have to return home from this trip, back to my life, back to reality.

After I get out of the shower, I pull on a pair of boxer shorts and a white tank top, then decide to send Nelli a text to check up on things. It's after six o' clock in the morning back home. The two of them are early risers so they should be up.

Me: Everything going okay?

It takes her a second to respond.

Nelli: Everything's fine. I even took her to the park and she enjoyed herself.

Me: Really? She usually hates leaving the house.

Nelli: I know. That's why I did it in baby steps. Took her in the car to get some ice cream first. Then we sat in the car at the park while we ate it. After a while, I convinced her to get out of the car and sit on the benches.

Go Nelli. I've tried countless times to get my mother to do more things, but to no avail. Maybe I suck at taking care of her more than I thought.

Nelli: I know what you're thinking and stop it. You're doing fine. I just have the magic touch. Now, enough about us. How are you? And why are you texting me so early?

Me: We just pulled over to get some sleep.

Nelli: At a hotel?

Me: Yeah, in Indiana somewhere.

Nelli: You're being careful, right?"

Me: Yep. Jax is a good driver and I always wear my seatbelt.

Nelli: I meant with the sex.

Oh, my God.

Me: With the sex? What does that even mean?

Nelli: It means you better be having him wrap it up.

Me: Ew, don't ever say that again.

Nelli: I have to. Someone has to look after you.

I start to tear up, thinking about when my mother was that someone. How when I was seventeen and decided I was going to lose my virginity, she took me to the doctor to get on the pill.

"I want you to be safe," she had said. "Make sure you're taken care of."

Now the roles are switched, and I'm the one taking her to the doctor for checkups and MRIs. I feel alone most days. Yes, I have Nelli, but that's about it.

I wipe away a few tears that manage to escape then text Nelli back.

Me: I'm being careful, okay. I have to go. Text or call if you need anything. Day or night.

Nelli: I will, just as long as you promise to have fun.

Me: Promise.

Nelli: Hugs and kisses, my Little Sunshine Girl.

My eyes bubble with more tears when she uses the nickname she used to call me back before life took over.

Me: Hugs and kisses Nelli Smelli.

Nelli: Nice one :)

I set the phone down on the sink, comb my damp hair, and put on some deodorant before leaving the bathroom. When I walk out, Jax is lying in bed on his back with his arm draped over his head and his eyes closed.

Maybe I've lucked out, and he's already fallen asleep.

I tiptoe over to the bed, kick off my flip-flops, then slip underneath the covers. I fluff the pillow, click off the lamp, and shut my eyes. Sleep feels impossible, though. I'm too wired. My pulse is soaring and the smell of Jax is sending my senses into a mad frenzy.

The sun is rising and soft trail light flows through the window and across Jax's naked chest. I have the most powerful urge to reach out and trace my fingers across his smooth flesh.

I wonder how far I'd have to go down before the feel of his skin would disappear… if he has pants on or not…

I consider peeking under the covers and wonder how big of a perv that makes me.

"Your heavy breathing's starting to creep me out."

Jax's voice startles me and I let out an absurd squeal. Slapping my hand over my mouth, I feel like an idiot.

Jax's eyelids lift open and his forehead creases. "Why the hell did you scream? Are you okay?"

I lower my hand from my mouth. "Yeah, you just scared me. I thought you were asleep."

"Were you watching me sleep?"

"No… and besides, you technically weren't asleep, just faking."

"You were watching me sleep." He smirks. "I'm not sure whether I should be creeped out or flattered."

I narrow my eyes. "I'd go with the first one, since I was really contemplating your murder."

"Yeah, right. I can tell you weren't."

"How?"

His gaze drops to my chest. "Because your nipples are perky as hell."

I glance down at my chest. Sure enough, without a bra on, the thin fabric of my tank top gives a clear view of how turned on I am.

He props up on his elbow with a cocky grin on his face. "We can pretend it's Friday if you need to."

I fight back a smile. "No thank you, Mr. Cocky."

His arrogance only increases. "If you don't like my cockiness, then you should probably lay off with the staring. Seriously Clara, you're stroking the crap out of my ego."

I roll my tongue in my mouth to keep from smiling and start to turn over onto my side. "We're not having sex tonight or on this trip, period."

His fingers enfold around my arms and he lures me toward him. "Who said anything about having sex. We do other things on Friday nights besides have sex."

I glance over at him. "Like what? Get ice cream?"

His eyes blaze with lust. "Don't you remember the first time we hooked up? How you got on your knees and took me in your mouth? That was kind of what started the whole thing to begin with."

"I was drunk when we did that," I lie as my cheeks flame. "I'm not usually like that."

"You were buzzed," he calls out my bullshit.

"You encouraged me," I retort, even though I was the one who instigated this whole thing between us. Who gave in to the attraction, who couldn't keep her hands to herself. Who was way too curious about what her friend would be like in bed. "You kept playing with my hair and saying all that stuff about my ass looking hot as hell."

"It does look hot as hell." He ravels a strand of my hair around his finger. "But you're lying. You know you started it. But that's okay. I wanted you just as much."

My entire body quivers from the sound of his raspy voice. "So you want me to give you head right now? You think that'll help me sleep better?" Sarcasm drips from my voice.

His eyes darken. "Nope. That's not what I'm suggesting at all."

"Good, because it seems like that'd only help *you* sleep."

A smile forms on his lips as he unravels my hair from his finger, shifts his weight toward me, and slides his body over mine. Then he nudges my legs apart, positions himself between them, and props an arm on each side of my head.

"Are you mad at me for doing this?" he asks, gazing down at me.

"That all depends on what this is." I sound breathless. My heart is thrashing in my chest and my mind is racing.

This is too intimate.

This isn't what you want.

He wouldn't even be doing this if he knew the whole truth about your life.

Think about the last time you were this close with someone. How Mack left and broke your heart.

"I'm not sure yet... I'm trying to figure out how much you trust me." He intently assesses my expression and my pulse accelerates.

You need to stop him.

Stop this before he kisses you, and you can't stop.

"I trust you a lot. Always have, but I don't think we should..." I trail off as he softly tastes my lips.

My body instantly curls into his warmth as my lips part and he slips his tongue into my mouth. My fingers delve into his flexed arms as I hold onto him, slowly biting his bottom lip, trying to give myself enough time to find the will to stop this. But then he groans and all my inhibitions melt.

I glide my hands down his arms, and then my fingers find their way to his taut stomach. His muscles flex as I feel his flesh, just like I thought about doing moments before. My hand travels downward to the top of his boxers and slips a hand under the waistband, but he reaches down and seizes my wrist, stopping me.

"No way," he breathes against my mouth.

"You're seriously stopping me?" I ask, astounded.

He nods his head up and down, breathing heavily. "I... have a plan." He pushes back, putting space between our mouths.

I jut out my lip, even though him ending the moment is probably a good thing. Doesn't help my horny body though.

"Relax," he says with reservation, like he's unsure of himself.

I open my mouth to ask him what he's doing, when his head suddenly moves downward. I may be inexperienced, but I'm not an idiot.

"Jax, we can't do that..." I trail off as he slides the bottom of my shirt up and places a delicate kiss on my tummy. His tongue quickly follows and he licks a path down to the waistband of my shorts. "Oh... my... God..." My muscles unwind as my hips arch upward and my eyes roll back in my head. "That feels... amazing..."

He lets out a soft, somewhat arrogant chuckle. Usually, I'd snap at him for being a cocky asshole, but he kisses me right below my belly button, and I can't form a single coherent thought. Even when he draws my shorts and panties down, I barely mutter an incoherent protest. He's never seen me this naked before. And I have a reason for being mostly dressed every time we fool around. But right now, I don't give a shit.

"You want me to stop?" Jax breathes raggedly as he spreads my legs open.

Unable to speak, I shake my head from side to side.

Moments later, I feel the warm caress of his lips between the center of my legs. Heat instantly bursts through my body and coils deep inside me. My muscles ravel with the first swipe of his tongue. I grip onto the blanket, desperate to hold onto something. I feel like I'm leaning over a cliff, about to fall into a place I've never been before. I'm terrified yet excited. Eager yet reluctant.

"Clara," Jax groans my name then drags his tongue down my center, "relax."

A gasp falters from my lips and I free the blanket from my hold and pull at the strands of his hair. All reservations suddenly melt, and the slow, calculated movements turn to untamed desire.

He licks and tugs and kisses as I writhe my hips against him. My body pulsates with need and my lungs struggle for oxygen as I drift farther away. My skin dampens and my mind empties. One last lick from his tongue

113

pushes me over the edge. I cry out Jax's name as I desperately tug at his hair, coming undone completely.

When I return to reality, Jax is kneeling between my legs and staring down at me. Strands of his brown hair are sticking up, probably from me pulling so hard.

"You okay?" His voice carries hesitancy.

I bob my head up and down. "Yeah, I'm fine." My voice sounds gravelly. "I've never done that before. It was... interesting."

The corners of his lips quirk. "Just interesting?"

I'm too tired to shrug. "And good."

"Interesting and good?" He presses his hand to his chest, appearing a little hurt. "Wow, I must have sucked."

Laughter escapes me, and even though it takes a lot of energy, I prop up on my elbows. "That's not what I meant."

"Then what did you mean?"

"That it was really, really fantastic. The best I've ever had."

"But you just said you'd never done that before."

"So? It was still fantastic."

"Good." He grins then leans down to kiss me.

I want to slide out from underneath him and put the barrier up between us again, but I'm too exhausted to move. At least, that's the reason I give myself. Deep down, I know there's more to it than that. There's a reason Jax is pretty much the only person who can make me smile anymore, who can make me laugh. Who can sneak past that wall I have around me. Because I care about him more than I want to admit.

I'll put the rules back into play tomorrow, I vow to myself as our lips connect. *I can't let this get out of hand. Can't let my heart get broken again.*

But as our lips connect and my body nearly trembles for his touch, I wonder if maybe I'm too late. The moment I agreed to this trip, I was pretty much agreeing to get closer to Jax. Eventually, I'm going to have to tell him what he's getting into.

I just hope he doesn't ruin me.

Chapter Seven

Jax

Eighteen hours after we leave the motel, Clara and I pull up to my childhood home. It looks worse than it did when I left—the entire neighborhood does. The siding is peeling off the two-story home, the porch is caving in, and the lawn is yellow and patchy. Someone has came and ripped up chunks of the concrete around the yard, for who knows what reason.

"This is home sweet home." I announce in a flat, unenthusiastic tone as I park the Jeep in the driveway.

"So, this is where you grew up?" Clara tentatively asks and I nod. She bites on her thumbnail as she studies the broken windows and shingles peeling off the roof.

Ever since we left the motel room, she's been acting torn over something. She hasn't been cold toward me or anything like that, but she's been stuck in some sort of internal battle over something ever since I spread her legs and

116

kissed her until she came apart. I didn't mean to take things that far with her. I was only messing around, figuring she'd stop me before I got too far, but she'd practically came undone just from me licking her stomach.

"Are you sure it's safe to go in?" Clara asks, plucking at the loose threads of her cutoff shorts.

I stare at the house, remembering all the rough, slightly insane people that have been in there. "Maybe I should go in first and check things out."

She glances around at the crumbling home next door. "I think I might feel safer being with you."

"Clara, I don't want you to worry." I unbuckle my seatbelt and reach over the console to tuck a strand of her hair behind her ear. "I won't let anything happen to you."

"I know you won't." Her fingers fold around the door handle. "But I want to go inside with you for support." She offers me a smile.

An emotional lump forms in my throat. "Okay, just stay close."

I get out of the car and meet her around the front. I lace my fingers through hers as we step up the rickety porch toward the front door. She doesn't pull away this time, probably because she's scared out of her damn mind.

Like the officer told me, the front door is busted in and hanging on one of the hinges.

"What happened to the door?" Clara gapes at the splintered wood of the doorframe.

"Someone probably kicked it in when my mother didn't answer. It happens sometimes." I squeeze her hand before stepping into the house.

The living room is exactly how I remember. Stained orange and brown carpet, broken glass on the floor, empty syringes everywhere. Alcohol bottles line the crooked stairway, and the air reeks of cigarette smoke and mold.

"You can go outside whenever you need to," I tell Clara when she draws the collar of her tank top over her nose.

"I'm fine," she assures me. "It just smells in here… like a dead animal or something."

I take a whiff of the air then wince. She's right. It does smell like something died in here. Adrenaline soars through my body when I realize what that could mean—it might not be a dead animal, but my mother's body rotting away.

"Wait here," I say then hurry through the house to track where the smell is coming from. Memories haunt me around every corner. So much happened in this place, so much bad stuff. Fights. Yelling. Drug use. Abuse.

By the time I reach the top of the stairway, I'm on the verge of throwing up. Not just from the smell, but because I'm remembering all the reasons I left.

I hate that I'm here again.

I check my mother's room, which has been cleared out; the bed and dresser are gone along with her clothes and all of her belongings. I peek into the room that used to be Avery's. All that's in there is a lumpy mattress on the floor and beer bottles. I stick my head into the bathroom and dry heave. The toilet has overflowed onto the floor, and the stench is enough to make my eyes water. I quickly shut the door. The dead animal smell has to be coming from inside there.

Still, I look inside the last room to be sure. My hands quiver as I grip the doorknob and enter my old bedroom. It looks exactly the same as I left it. Even the dresser is still tipped over from when my mother's then husband tried to throw it at me.

I swallow hard as the memory of that day rushes over me. Lester swung his fist and I swung back. Blood painted our knuckles. He kept shouting for me to respect him, that I had to because he was my father. He wasn't my real father, though. He was my fifth stepfather and acted like he was the man of the house, even though he was a blip on a long list of men my mother let into her home. In his words, he was the boss and made the rules, even if the rules he set were fucked up and warped. What really sucked is that I didn't—and still don't even know who my real father is. Even my mother doesn't. Men like Lester are all I've ever known when it comes to fathers.

"Are you okay?" Clara unexpectedly moves up behind me and gently places a hand on my shoulder.

I'm so lost in the memory I jolt from her touch. "Yeah, I'm fine." She pulls away as I face her. "I'm just thinking about stuff."

"About your mom?" she asks.

I shake my head. "About what happened the last time I was here."

"Oh, the fight?"

I free a shaky breath. "It happened in here."

When I nod my head at the room behind me, she scans the messy area, the holes in the walls, the cracks in the ceiling, the broken window. "Was this your bedroom?" she asks.

I run my thumb along the ring on my finger, thinking about the time my mother gave it to me, the one happy moment I ever had in this place. "It was."

Sorrow fills her expression. "Jax, I'm so sorry."

"For what?" I ask. She has nothing to be sorry about. She came with me on this trip, is making being in this house bearable.

"That you had to live here." She threads our fingers together. "I didn't realize... that it was this bad for you."

"I tried to warn you. This is why I asked you not to judge me." *Please, please, don't let her judge me.*

"I know you did, but this," she glances around the room again, noting the holes in the walls, "is more than I'm capable of imagining."

"That's a good thing." I sketch my fingers along her jawline and think about kissing her, knowing if I did, I'd probably feel a little better. She's even holding my hand, so I'm betting I could get away with stealing a kiss. But it seems wrong to do something I love so much when we're standing in the midst of a crackhouse. "We should go get checked into a motel, get something to eat, then start asking around to see if anyone's seen her." I start for the stairway, pulling her with me. "We need to move fast since we only have three days here before we have to head back."

She nods in agreement. "Do you have an idea of where to start? I mean, who to ask. Or are you just going to wing it?"

121

"I have a few ideas of where to start," I reply as we descend the stairs, the steps creaking under our weight. "But I'm going to warn you in advance that pretty much every place we go is going to be as bad as here. In fact, you might want to stay in the motel room or hang around town."

She hesitates, as if she's actually considering doing it. Part of me of is glad that she is. Somehow I'd forgotten how bad this place is. But then she straightens her stance.

"No, I'm going with you. You shouldn't go through this alone."

"Are you sure?" I give a pressing glance at the drug paraphernalia on the floor. "I won't be upset if you don't want to. In fact, I'd kind of prefer if you didn't."

"Jax, you asked me to come so you wouldn't have to be alone in this, right?" she asks, and I unwillingly nod. "Okay, then. I'm going with you."

"All right, but only if you promise me one thing."

"And what's that?"

"If at any point things start to get dangerous, you bail. I don't want anything happening to you."

She nods, looking worried.

I want to tell her everything will be okay. That I'm just being overly careful. Nothing bad is going to happen. But I don't want to lie to her.

I lived this life for too damn long and know how dangerous things can get.

Chapter Eight

Clara

"Okay, this place isn't too bad." I bounce down on the queen size bed in the motel room.

After seeing where Jax lived, I was expecting a lot worse, but the motel seems to be in the better side of town and could probably pass for at least three stars. Add that to the fact that I just got a text from Nelli saying she actually took my mother to a restaurant for lunch, and I'm feeling pretty okay right now.

Jax shoves the keycard into his wallet. "This is the best place in town."

My expression plummets as I kneel up on the bed. "I hope you didn't fork out a lot of money just so I'd feel safe. Please tell me you didn't."

"It wasn't that much." He empties the spare change from his pocket and dumps it onto the nightstand.

"Jax—" I start to object.

But he talks over me. "So, there's this drive-in diner place like a mile away from here that has the best hamburgers ever. I was thinking we could stop there then head out to this motel my mother sometimes hangs out at. It's on the other side of town."

"Why does she hang out at a motel?" I ask as I put my hair up into a ponytail.

He avoids eye contact with me, staring out the window. "It's where she goes to make money."

I climb off the bed. "Doing what?"

His shoulders lift and fall as he exhales heavily. "Whoring herself out basically." He looks so ashamed about the fact, even though I already knew his mother is a prostitute.

I want to hug the pain away, wrap my arms around him and tell him everything will be okay. I remember, after my father died, how much I wished someone would hug me and assure me everything would turn out all right. No one ever did, though, and it really wouldn't have mattered in the long run, wouldn't have changed anything.

I wrap my arms around myself and move up behind him. "Are you going to be okay with this?"

He has asked me the same question like a hundred times, when really he should be worrying about himself more. The agony in his eyes when he entered that home made me want to cry. And the condition of that house… I'd thought my apartment was bad, but that place… No one should have to live under those conditions. And Jax grew up in it.

"I'm fine," He stares at the greying sky stretching across the town. "We should probably get going, though. We're running out of daylight."

"You make us sound like vampires," I joke in an attempt to make him smile.

"Another fantasy of yours? You want me to bite you tonight?" His lips twitch in amusement.

I want to tell him no but I also don't want to ruin the moment. "No way. I'm the boss," I play along, "therefore, the biter."

"That's no fair. You always get to be the boss." He fakes a pout, looking so adorable and sexy it's ridiculous.

"No way. You were the boss the other night. *Remember?*"

"How do you figure that?"

"Because you're the one who," I motion downward at my thigh area, "you know."

"No, I don't know." He taps his finger against his bottom lip. "Guess you'll just have to say it aloud."

I give him a playful shove and laugh.

A second or two ticks by, and then he cocks his brow. "I'm still waiting for you to fill me in on what you're talking about. What did I do the other night that made me the boss?"

"Oh, my God, you're such a smartass sometimes." I collect my purse from the chair and head for the door. "Come on. I'm starving."

"So am I," he says, following after me.

Although I'm pretty sure a sexual innuendo is hidden in his comment, I choose to ignore it.

"So, a drive-in diner, huh?" I sling the handle of my bag over my shoulder as we step out of the room. "Does that mean the waitresses are wearing roller skates and short little shorts."

"Why? Would that turn you on if they did?"

"Jax," I hiss as the breezy Wyoming air bites at my skin. The sun is descending behind the mountains enclosing the town, and the later it gets, the lower the temperature seems to drop. "Seriously, can we lay off with the dirty talk for like maybe an hour?"

"I could try, but it kind of relaxes me." He yanks on the door, making sure it's shut all the way, and then we cross the parking lot toward his Jeep. When I shoot him a doubtful look, he says, "What? It helps distract me, at least it does with you."

"Aw crap. You can't give me an answer like that."

He cocks his head to the side. "Why not?"

"Because now I have to let you."

His eyes glimmer mischievously. "Did I just get a free pass to say whatever I want?"

"Maybe." My frown deepens at my response.

He rubs his hands together. "Wow, where to start? There's so many things running through my head right now…" His gaze darts to a woman strutting toward us. She's wearing a leopard print dress that leaves hardly anything to the imagination, neon pink stilettoes, and her brown hair has a matching streak down the front strand.

"Fuuuck," Jax curses under his breath, jerking his hand roughly through his hair as he kicks a rock across the parking lot.

"Is that your mom?" I ask, even though the woman looks too young to be his mother.

Jax grudgingly shakes his head. "No… it's one of my ex-girlfriends. Please, for the love of God, don't judge me on what's about to happen."

Before I can even process what he just said, Miss Leopard Print reaches us.

"Well, well, well, look what the dog dragged in." She flashes her yellow teeth as she grins. "Jax Hensley, what the hell have you been up to? I haven't seen you in forever."

Jax tensely rubs the back of his neck. "That's because I moved to North Carolina a couple of years ago."

"Really?" Her bloodshot eyes widen in astonishment. "How come I didn't know about this?"

Jax shrugs, his arm falling to his side. "I didn't really tell anyone when I left."

"Well, that's cool, I guess. We all need to get away sometimes." Her eyes flick to me then back to Jax. "Are you moving back?

"Fuck no," he answers sharply. When the woman flinches, he offers her an apology. "Sorry, Bev, I didn't mean to sound like such an ass. It's just that... Have you by chance seen my mom?"

She squints one eye as she thinks. "You know what? I think the last time I saw her she was down at the Dirty Tiger. That was about a week or two ago."

"The Dirty Tiger?" I don't mean to say it aloud, but the name is just too ridiculous.

Bev stares at me with her face screwed in puzzlement.

"Oh, Bev this is Clara, my," he glances at me, "my friend I guess."

"Your friend you guess," Bev states with skepticism, focusing back on Jax. "Since when do you have female friends?" Her tongue slips out of her mouth and wets her chapped lips. "Because the Jax I remember didn't use girls for friends. He just fucked them."

I fight back a gag. But seriously, the idea of Jax being with this woman who has track marks on her arms and teeth rotting out of her head makes me want to hurl. He said not to judge him, so I'm trying to keep an open mind, but it's hard.

"Sorry," she offers me an apology.

"It's cool," I reply, even though I'm lost as to what she's apologizing for.

"So, the Dirty Tiger," Jax interrupts with disdain in his tone. "That's where she's hanging out now?"

Bev nods, still gawking at me. "Yeah, but like I said, that was a week or two ago."

"Dammit, I really fucking hate that place," Jax says heavy heartedly.

"It's not that bad." Bev finally rips her gaze off me.

"You used to not think that." Jax elevates his brows at Bev's outfit.

She lifts her chin. "Hey, I do what I gotta do to survive. Don't judge me just because you got out of this shithole."

"I'm not judging you," he tells her. "I just think you're better than this."

"Well, I'm not." She shoves her hand at him. "Do you have any extra cash you can spare? I'm running low."

"I'm not giving money to you so you can buy drugs." Jax's gaze fleetingly drops to the circular bluish and purple splotches on Bev's forearm.

"Whatever." She crosses her arms and spins on her heels. "Thanks for wasting my time." She stomps toward the front area of the motel with her heels crunching against the gravel.

"Well, she's a real gem," I mutter after she's out of hearing range.

"She wasn't like that when I was dating her," Jax explains as we head toward his vehicle again. "But I'm not surprised she ended up where she has."

I feel a little better knowing Bev wasn't that way when Jax dated her, but the last thing he said is unsettling. "Why aren't you surprised she turned into a junkie?"

"Because that's just the way things work in The Subs." Jax stuffs his hand into his pocket to retrieve the car keys. "The people born there generally get sucked into the environment."

"The Subs?" I ask as he unlocks the passenger door.

"It's the nickname people around here gave to the area south of the highway." He motions to the left of us. "Basically, it's the shitty area of town where more than half the residents do drugs or sell drugs or sell themselves for drugs."

"And it's where you grew up? And Bev?" I move around him to get into the car, but stop before I hop in. "You say the people that live there generally get stuck in the environment, but you and Avery didn't."

"Yeah, well, we're kind of unique cases. Avery escaped this life, but not without a lot of bumps in the road first and me... And me, well, I was sick of having complications in my life, so I fucking ran and never looked back. I just wanted to live for once, you know."

"Yeah, I know," I say hoarsely, thinking about how I used to have the same attitude. 'Live life in the moment' was my motto. I had plans to travel after I graduated. Plans to do something amazing with my life. So many plans and none of them happened.

"What's wrong?" he asks, noting the croak in my voice.

"Nothing." I clear my throat. "And you're not just a unique case. You're a special case, Jax. You've completely turned your life around."

He places a hand on the car just to the side of my head and angles his body toward me until only a few inches are between us. "If I didn't know any better, I'd guess you just gave me a compliment."

"It's a good thing you know better," I retort, but my voice is unsteady as his body heat seeps into my skin.

"I guess so." He eyes me over for an unbearable amount of time before he pushes back. "It looks like we're hitting up the Dirty Tiger after the diner."

I pull a repulsed face as I slide my butt into the seat. "The name sounds so gross, like a advertisement for

STD's. Come on in to the Dirty Tiger, where you walk in with a smile on your face and leave with herpes between your legs."

Laughter bursts from his lips. "You know, as funny as that is, it's actually pretty close to the truth."

"So disgusting." I stick out my tongue and gag.

"Relax. Just don't use the toilets or let any dicks into your pussy, and you'll be fine."

My lips part in shock, and I reach out to swat him. "You're so vile."

He skitters out of my reach, laughing his ass off. "You're the one who brought up herpes."

Okay, he has me there. "Fine, I'll hold my bladder and try my best to stay away from all penises."

"Good idea. Although, I'm not sure if the penises will be able to stay away from you." When I glare at him, he adds, "I'm kidding… but not really." His finger traces below my eye, causing my eyelashes to flutter. "You're too beautiful and are going to stand out like a sore thumb in a place like the Dirty Tiger." His mouth tugs to a lopsided grin, and then he heads around the car to get inside.

I shut the door, release a weighted breath, and briefly close my eyes. My heart is pounding from his touch, and my skin tingles everywhere.

Flirting. Smiles. Laughs. Hand holding. What the hell have I gotten myself into?

On our way home, I'll set boundaries again, I tell myself, ignoring the fact that I keep bending the rules the more time I spend with Jax.

At the rate things are going, this will end in a disaster like it did with Mack. Jax will run the other way when he discovers the truth about my life. Like he said himself, he doesn't want complications in his life. And my life is one big, messy, stressful complication.

Chapter Nine

Jax

After we get some hamburgers at the retro diner, we make the short drive to the outskirts of town. A very, very cheap strip/dance club located on the side of the freeway, the Dirty Tiger has a fitting name.

Clara shudders as she assesses the metal building lit up by neon signs promising a good time. The windows are grimy, blocking the view to the inside, but that's probably for the better.

"Wow, it's worse than I imagined," she mumbles as she stares at the corner of the building where a man is leaning back, and a woman is down on her knees. Despite being partially hidden in the shadows, it's pretty clear what they're doing.

"Maybe I should take you back to the motel then come back by myself," I suggest, unbuckling my seatbelt.

As terrified as Clara looks, she shakes her head. "No, I'm going in there with you."

"Are you sure? Because it's going to be way worse inside. I don't want to be the reason you're subjected to the hard shit in life."

"My father died right in front of me… I already know about the hard shit in life," she mutters then pushes open the door and jumps out before I can say anything.

Jesus, I knew her father died, but not in front of her.

I hurry after her. It feels like I should say something, but I can't figure out what. We make it halfway across the gravel parking lot before I speak again.

"I didn't know that about your father. That must have been hard." I splay my fingers across the small of her back as we near the entrance of the club.

People are loitering around, drinking, and chatting. I can feel Clara's tension through her knotted muscles.

"It was in the beginning, but I'm okay now. I mean, it still hurts and everything when I think about it, but it doesn't eat away at me every day or anything." She hovers close to me when a guy wearing leather pants walks by us, checking her out. "Look, I'm sorry I brought that up. I don't even know why I said it." She halts a few feet from the door and looks at me in desperation. "I'm just so confused being here with you, seeing your world… learning so much about you. It's starting to feel so wrong that I know so much about you, and you hardly know anything about me."

"So, then tell me."

She casts a wary glance at the club. "*Here*?"

I shake my head. "Not here, but maybe when we get back to the motel or on the way back home to North Carolina."

"I don't think that's a wise idea," she utters quietly.

"Why not?" I question. What is she so afraid of? I wish I knew. Wish she'd open up to me so I could help her get past her fear.

Her eyes fill with panic. "This trip is about helping you find your mother, not about my problems. I swear I didn't mean for that to slip out. It's just that when I'm with you... I get confused."

"About what?"

"Stuff."

She's being evasive, which I guess is normal for her, except she finally brought up her family, only to drop the subject immediately.

"First of all, you can always tell me anything, anytime, day or night," I explain, hoping she won't shut down. "And second, this trip isn't just about me. Yeah, we're here to find out where my mother is, but I wanted you to come with me so I could spend time with you. We hardly ever get to spend time together, even when we were friends."

"We're still friends, though. Right?"

"Right." I sound as confused as she looks. I want to push her for more details about her life, have her spill her soul to me, but this is hardly the fucking place to do that. "Let's go inside and get this over with. Then we can talk some more when we get back to the room. How does that sound?"

Without responding, she steps back so I can open the door. Grabbing her hand, we enter the club. Her fingers constrict as the hazy atmosphere swallows us. Classic rock plays from the stereo and vibrates the floor littered with cigarette butts. The smoky air smells like severely bad body odor mixed with cheap beer and a hint of dirty sex. The room is filled mostly with men, but a few women are hanging out by the tables and dancing around a stained pole onstage.

"I feel like I need to take a shower just from walking in here!" she hollers over the music.

"Agreed!" I nod toward the bar area. "Let's make this quick!"

139

We push our way through the crowd and up to the counter where it's a little bit quieter. I lift my hand to flag the bartender down. When he turns around, I recognize the middle-aged, stocky guy. I don't know whether to be relieved or disappointed about that fact.

"Since when do you work here?" I ask Joe, my old little league coach. I haven't seen him since I tried out for sports in an attempt to get away from the house more. Turns out, though, I sucked at athletic stuff.

A shocked grin spreads across his face when he realizes who I am. "Holy shit, Jax Hensley. I haven't seen you since…"

"Since baseball season when I was eleven," I finish for him, feeling a little more at ease.

"How the hell have you been? It's been forever." He glances at Clara who's practically clutching my side.

"Good. I'm living in North Carolina now and go to college." I nod my head in Clara's direction. "This is Clara, one of my friends from there."

Clara nervously waves at him. "It's nice to meet you."

"The pleasure's all mine." His attention lands back on me, and he shakes his head in awe. "Wow, I can't believe you got out of here and made it to college. That's fucking fantastic, Jax. Seriously. Really great."

"Thanks." The music shifts to an upbeat pop song and the lights on the stage wildly flash. "So, do you work here now?"

Joe sighs as he places two shot glasses on the counter. "Unfortunately, yes."

Clara inches closer to me when an older guy shoots her a toothless grin from across the bar. "Jax, please hurry up," she whispers softly enough only I can hear. "I'm freaking out. I think the guy over there might be plotting a herpes attack on me."

I choke on a cough then clear my throat. "How'd that happened?" I ask Joe as I slip my arm around Clara's back and draw her closer. "The last time I saw you, you were working at the sporting goods store."

He selects a bottle of tequila from the shelf behind him and untwists the cap. "Yeah, this is what happens when you're stupid enough to have an affair with your boss. Divorce is ugly, my friend. And so is getting fired." He fills up the shot glass with the golden liquid and returns the bottle back to the shelf. "First shots are on me."

"Thanks." I glance at Clara. "You want a drink? It might help you relax."

She looks like she could use ten drinks. She promptly snatches up the shot, throws her head back, and devours the liquid. "Thanks," she says to Joe as she places the glass on the counter.

"Anytime." He collects the shot glasses and sets then with the rest of the dirty glasses.

A guy walks up to the counter and orders two beers, and Joe heads to the tap.

"So, I actually came here for a reason," I say to Joe while Clara grabs my shot and downs it too. "I'm looking for my mom. Have you seen her?"

He aligns a tall glass under the beer tap and begins filling it up. "I saw her hanging around the backstage area about a week ago, but she was only here for about five minutes."

"Does she work here?" I glance over my shoulder at the stage. A woman who is twirling around upside down on the bar looks close to my mother's age, so the possibility seems plausible.

He shakes his head as he puts two beers down on counter in front of the guy who ordered them. "No, she just hangs around sometimes." He collects the cash from the guy and stuffs the tip into a jar. "But Larry, the owner finally threw her out last week because she was harassing the clients."

"What exactly do you mean by harassing?"

He opens the register and stuffs the dollar bills inside. "She was asking people for money and kept yammering about how, if they didn't help her, she was going to be a dead woman."

Clara's arms tighten around my waist, and she presses against my side. She starts tracing circles on my back, like she's trying to soothe me.

As I think of the message my mother left me five days ago, it feels like the wind is knocked out of me. "You haven't seen her since she got kicked out?"

Joe shakes his head as he rests his arms on the counter. "Look, Jax, I'm not sure why you came back here, but if you're smart you'll walk out that door and drive back to North Carolina. You don't want to get involved in the shit your mother's involved in."

"I need to know she's okay before I can leave." I stand my ground. "So, if you know where she is, just tell me."

Pity fills his eyes. "All I know is that she was in trouble with a guy named Marcus Dalemaring."

"Marcus Dalemaring?" The Marcus my mother mentioned on the voice mail. "I don't know who that is."

"You wouldn't. He showed up here about a year ago and has gotten a pretty good rep for selling drugs and hiring out prostitution." Joe pushes back from the counter. "From what I understand, your mother was helping him with his business."

"You mean she was one of his prostitutes?" I shake my head. Things never change with her. "Or was it drugs this time?"

"I think she brought in new clients for him," he explains as he picks up a rag. "And from what I understand, that involved her in a lot of money transactions, so I'm pretty sure you can piece together what happened."

"Who the hell would trust her with money?"

"A pimp and a drug dealer," he explains as he scrubs down the dirty counters. "Especially one who hasn't lived here long enough to know your mother's reputation for fucking over people."

"So, she screwed him over, and he threatened to kill her," I mumble, realizing how right my aunt was when she said my mother was probably dead in a ditch somewhere. The harsh reality painfully sinks in. She really might be dead this time. I knew it could be a possibility, but I'm suddenly realizing how likely of an outcome it could be.

"That's just what I heard, but who knows exactly what happened."

"Do you have any idea where I can find this Marcus Dalemaring guy?"

"No." He drapes the rag over his shoulder. "And, even if I did, I wouldn't tell you. Get in your car and go home, Jax." With that, he turns his back to me and walks off toward the storage area.

"Now what do we do?" Clara stares up at me with concern.

"Now we go." I gently nudge her toward the door.

"But what about your mom?" she asks as she tucks in her elbows and squeezes past people.

"We'll keep looking for her tomorrow, but right now, I need to get you back to the hotel. It's already way past dark." I steer her through the crowd and out the door.

We both inhale the fresh air the moment we step outside.

"I'm going to have to do a body inspection when I get home," Clara says as I usher her past gawkers. "Make sure I didn't contract something solely from the air. It smelled like I was breathing STD's."

"Yeah..." I'm distracted by my thoughts as I try to figure out what to do next.

Keep asking around until I find this Marcus guy? Go home like Joe insisted I should?

"All right." Clara grinds to a halt and stops me with her. "Tell me what you're thinking because I know you have to be thinking about something important for you to pass up commenting on my body inspection remark."

"I'm just trying to figure out what to do next. If I should go home or not."

"Do you want to go home?"

"I don't know. What do you think?"

"You really want to know?" she asks and I nod. "I think we drove a long way out here to find out what happened to her, because it was eating up at you not knowing. I think, if we go back now without figuring out where she is, it'll drive you crazy."

She's right. If I went back home right now, what happened to my mother would haunt me, maybe even for the rest of my life.

"You're right. I think we should stay." I lace our fingers together and head for the car again. "But on one condition."

She's staring down at our interlocked hands, looking puzzled as hell. "And what's that?"

"That when we get back to the motel, you'll let me help you with your body inspection."

She looks up at me and rolls her eyes, but doesn't comment or try to swat me. In fact, she seems like she briefly considers letting me.

I bite back a smile. "If I didn't know any better, I'd think you might want that to happen."

Now she moves in for the swat, but I capture her hand and jerk her against my body. I've had such a shitty night and all I want to do is not feel shitty. Being with Clara does that for me. I want her, even though it's not Friday. I want her in my car, in the motel room, everywhere. All the time. Every day.

Even though I know she'll get upset, I lean down and let my mouth linger on hers, waiting for her to pull back and end the kiss. Instead, she parts her lips. I don't know why she does it. Perhaps she feels bad for me. I don't care what the reason is.

I slide my arms around her, press her body against mine, and kiss her deeply. Our mouths move slowly and I savor each breathless whimper she makes. She tastes like tequila with a hint of French fries and the feel of her body heat nearly smothers me in the best way possible. I don't come up for air until she moans out my name and I have to stop; otherwise, I'm going to rip off her clothes right here in the parking lot.

When we break apart, she doesn't say anything. She simply turns and hurries for the car as if she's terrified out of her Goddamn mind.

I just wish I knew what she's afraid of.

Being with me?

Or is it something else?

Chapter Ten

Clara

By the time we're driving back to the motel, it's past ten o'clock. Pretty early compared to my normal bedtime, but all I can think about doing is lying down and shutting my eyes.

That kiss took a lot out of me emotionally. I'd forgotten how intense a kiss could be when it isn't linked to sex or foreplay. Kissing just to kiss usually has meaning behind it. That kiss Jax and I shared definitely meant something, but I can't figure out exactly what.

Okay, who am I kidding? Everything we've done has meant something. I've just been living in denial. My heart is about to get broken again. I can feel it in the pit of my stomach, a gnawing ache that won't go away.

To distract myself from my thoughts, I send a text to Nelli. When she doesn't respond right away, I start to panic and end up calling her even though Jax is in the car with me and will be able to hear everything that's said. I just keep thinking about all the times my mom tried to wander out of the house at night. What if she got the door unlocked and made it out without Nelli knowing?

"Clara, what's wrong?" Nelli answers after four rings, sounding exhausted.

"I tried to text you, but you didn't respond." I turn toward the window, trying to keep the conversation as private as I can.

"That's because I was asleep." When she yawns into the receiver, the two hour time difference dawns on me, that it's after midnight back in North Carolina.

"Oh shit, Nelli, I'm so sorry," I apologize, feeling horrible. "I forgot how late it is there."

"It's okay. I needed to wake up and check on your mom, anyways."

"How's she doing?"

"Good. She even helped me bake a cake for Mr. Garlifed and went with me to take it to him."

"You didn't return with any roosters, did you?"

"Nope," she assures me. "Well, not that I'm aware of."

I rub my heavy eyelids. "Good. I'm glad everything's going okay."

"Are you okay? You sound either tired or upset... I can't tell which."

"Tired," I tell her through a yawn. "It's been a long couple of days."

"I bet it has." She pauses. "How's everything going with the safeness?"

I give a sidelong glance in Jax's direction. "I thought we agreed not to talk about that ever again."

"And I thought I made it pretty clear that was never going to happen."

"Fine, yes, the safeness is going well." I can feel Jax's eyes burning holes in the side of my head. "I'll let you go now. Sorry for waking you up."

"No problem, Clara... Stellar. Call me if you need anything."

"Clara Stellar? You're slacking."

"I'm tired, but I'll do better next time."

"All right, Nelli Tiserelli. Talk to you later." I hang up then slump back in the seat.

Jax is watching me intensely. "Who's Nelli?" he wonders as he flips the brights on.

"Huh?" *Did I say her name out loud?*

"You said Nelli on the phone." He treads cautiously. "I know that's not your mom's name."

Jessica Sorensen

My phone clanks as I drop it into the console. I try to conjure up a lie, but I'm so tired my mind blanks out on me. "She's my aunt."

He cranks down the volume of the stereo. "You called your aunt… Why?" There's a speck of insinuation in his tone, probably because I rarely mention my family.

"She's staying with my mom while I'm gone." I can tell he wants to ask questions, so I add, "This kind of falls into the stuff I don't want to tell you about."

"But I thought we agreed we were going to talk more about that stuff when we made it back to the motel room."

"I don't think we ever agreed to that."

"I'm pretty sure we did," he replies.

We're quiet the rest of the way back to the motel and I sink into my thoughts about what exactly he expects to happen once we get to the motel room. Does he think I'm going to just pour my soul out to him? Just like that? Then what? He realizes what a mess my life is and ignores me until we get home, then sends me on my way. I'll end up alone again, with no one, with no Jax. And I like having my Jax, even if the time we have together is limited and rule restricted.

My mind is unbelievably wired during the drive, but by the time we make it to the room, I start to crash. All I want to do is pass out.

"Road trips are exhausting," I mutter as I kick my sandals off and flop face first onto the mattress. "I just want to go to sleep."

"Then go to sleep," Jax replies as he closes the door and flips the lock.

I twist my head toward him. "I have to shower first and wash the Dirty Tiger stench off me. Plus, I'm not sure I can actually fall asleep. My mind's too wired with thoughts of dirty stripper poles and toothless, pervy men."

"How about this." He drops his wallet and keys onto the nightstand then climbs onto the bed with me. "You go take a bath while I go raid the vending machine? Then we can stream a movie until you fall asleep." He swings a leg over me to straddle my back then places his hands on my shoulders and starts massaging my sore muscles.

My eyes widen, and I open my mouth to protest, but it feels so incredible the words get lost in my moan.

Jax chuckles. "Or we could just spend all night doing this."

"I might take you up on that offer," I murmur, burying my face into the comforter and stretching out my arms. I wonder if he's going to drop the subject of me telling him stuff. Could I be that lucky? "That feels so good."

His fingers delve deeper, kneading and working magic on my back. The longer the massage goes on, the louder I moan. It's absurdly intimate but feels way too good for me to ask him to stop.

"Clara, if you keep making those noses, I'm going to lose it." His voice is raspy, nearly cracking.

"Huh…?" I barely comprehend what he's saying as I float away to a soothing place I haven't been to in three years.

I miss being so relaxed. How in the hell is it possible to get lost in someone's touch like this, to the point where reality doesn't even seem real anymore?

He shifts his weight and I feel his breath against my neck. His fingers continue to work, tracing circles on the bare flesh of my shoulders. "I think I owe you a bite, right?" he whispers huskily then his teeth graze my lobe.

My body convulses uncontrollably, and I clutch onto the comforter for dear life. "I think it was the other way around." I open my eyes and meet his hungry gaze. "I was the one who was supposed to bite you."

"I'm pretty sure that was never fully decided."

"Guess we'll both have to do it then." Before I can back out, I flip onto my back and lift my mouth to his neck. I lightly graze my teeth across his neck and smile when he shivers.

After he regains control over himself, he seizes my wrists and pins my arms beside my head. "I thought you were tired?" he asks breathlessly as my chest arches against his.

I shrug, but with my hands trapped above me, the movement is awkward. "You woke me up with the bite."

A smile expands across his face. "You want me to bite you again?"

No. "Yes." *What the hell is wrong with me?*

He seems as shocked by my response as I am, but dips his head and gently nips at the sensitive spot just below my ear.

"Mmm…" I hum with a shiver. When his tongue slips out, and he licks a path down my neck, I damn near lose it. "Jax." I stab my fingers into his hands, which are still holding down my arms.

"What?" His voice is innocent enough, but he rocks his body against mine in a very not-so-innocent way.

I gasp as his hardness presses between my legs and heat courses through my body. "It's not Friday," I breathe stupidly.

"You're really going to hold onto that still?" He's mildly amused. And one-hundred percent turned on.

"Maybe... I don't know..."

He takes that as a go ahead, and his lips crash down on mine. Our tongues twine, our breaths mix, and our bodies align perfectly. With his hands still holding my arms against the mattress, he rolls his hips against mine. I hitch my legs around his waist, giving him more access as he kisses me until I'm lightheaded and breathless.

He lets go of one of my wrists, and his hand travels across the outside of my shirt, along my ribcage and to my breast. My nipples harden underneath my shirt. Through the thin fabric, I know he can feel it.

"I want to see you...all of you..." he whispers as he devours me with his lips. "Clara, tell me I can." When I don't reply, he gently pinches my nipple.

A cry claws up my throat as heat jolts through my body.

"Tell me I can take your shirt off," he practically begs.

I want to tell him yes. Want him to keep doing what he's doing. Want him inside me. But I'm too afraid to cross that intimate line yet.

With a soft bite of my bottom lip, he grunts then pulls away, leaving my body aching as he sits back on the bed

"What are you doing?" I whine, pushing up on my elbows.

He combs his fingers through his tousled hair, his eyes fastened on the floor. "I want to talk."

"*Talk?* Right now?" I pout out my bottom lip.

He chuckles, but his laughter swiftly dissipates when he looks up at me. The determination smoldering in his hazel eyes causes me to shrink back. "I know we have all these rules. You say you don't have time for a relationship, but it feels like I hardly know you, and you know so much about me." He scoots closer, takes my hand in his, and delicately sketches the folds of my fingers. "I want to get to know you."

I stare at our hands, struggling with whether to pull away or not. "You know more about me than most people do."

"But you haven't told me anything about your home life. Hell, I just learned about your father."

157

"But is that really even important? I mean, it just doesn't seem like something you have to know."

"I guess that all depends." He smashes his lips together, upset.

"On what?" I ask, wanting more than anything to erase the hurt from his eyes. I've already seen him too upset today.

"On what this is," his gaze falls to our hands, "what our relationship means to you. Because whether or not you want me to feel anything for you, I do. I pretty much have since the first day I met you."

My head bobbles back as I groan in mortification. "God, don't remind me of that day. I have no idea why you didn't run like hell the other way."

"Are you kidding me?" He tucks a lock of my hair behind my ear. "That was the most real I've ever seen you. Well, up until last night." He cracks a joke at the end, but I can tell he's nervous by his wobbly voice.

"I looked hideous."

"You never look hideous."

I sit up straight, crisscross my legs, and sigh. I knew this was coming. The inevitable. And I have two choices.

Keep running until I reach a dead end.

Or tell Jax my story and slam head on into the dead end.

I think about what my dad would tell me to do. He'd say stop running, that it does no good and only drains the energy out of you. I want to be that person again. The fearless person I once was.

So I summon a deep breath and prepare my heart for another break.

"I wasn't lying when I said I don't have time for a relationship," I start unsteadily. "I have so many responsibilities I sometimes can't keep up with them."

"Like work and school?"

"Work. School. My mom." I pick at my fingernails to avoid looking at him. "Not only did I lose my father in the accident, but I pretty much lost my mom. I mean, she's alive and everything but she has brain damage and is pretty much like a kid." I blow out an uneven breath as my heart violently pounds inside my chest. It's been so long since I spoke aloud about this stuff with anyone. *Breathe, Clara. Breathe.* "My sister pretty much bailed on me after the funeral, says it's too painful to talk to me anymore because I remind her of everything she lost. But it wouldn't have mattered if she stuck around. I promised my dad right before he died that I'd take care of my mother." I don't look

159

up at him as I speak, too afraid his eyes will match Mack's the day I told him how my life was going to be. "Between work, taking care of my mom, school, and paying bills, I just don't have time for other things. Plus, it's really not fair to bring someone into that mess."

He remains quiet for a while, dragging his finger along the ring he wears. When he'd told me the story about where he got it, I wanted to cry. It's the only present his mother ever gave him, and there was such sadness in his tone.

"What do you mean by it isn't fair?" His voice is gentler than I expected it to be.

I shrug, letting my hands fall to my lap. "I don't know. Most people our age don't want that. I mean, I can't go to parties all the time. I spend most of my nights either working the nightshift or making sure my mother doesn't try to escape the house. My days are filled with laundry, cooking, cleaning, paying bills, and chasing roosters out of the house."

"It sounds a lot like my sister's life," he says, his tone light. "Well, minus the rooster. Although, one time, Mason did bring home a hamster. We're still not sure where he got it from."

"Yeah, which kind of proves my point. I mean, I remember how excited you were when Avery got her new job and you were able to do more things. Being with me would take that away."

"That's not the same thing. Avery is my sister, and while I don't mind helping her out, I kind of want my own life."

"I know." I finally dare to meet his gaze then instantly regret it. His eyes are so intense, so overwhelming, so compassionate. Not at all what I was expecting. "Being with me… you wouldn't have that." My eyes start to burn as I say similar words Mack uttered to me. "I'd ruin your life."

"Why? Because you have to take care of your mom? You have to work? Be responsible? That's called life, Clara." He cups my face between his hands. "And yeah, yours is a little more complicated than others but so what. That doesn't make me want to be with you any less."

"But you said that's why you left here… because you didn't want a complicated life."

"You misunderstood me." He pauses, searching for the right words. "All my life, complications have been forced on me. I was born into a world where I had to grow up fast. When I finally escaped that life, I had to live with my sister. While I love Mason, I kind of felt obligated to help her because she helped take care of me. This thing between us… whatever you want it to be… I'm *choosing* it. Choosing to make my life complicated because I think it's worth it."

Tears drip from my eyes. "You want to choose it? After what I just told you?"

He swipes the pad of his thumb across my cheeks, erasing the tears. "Who on earth wouldn't choose you?"

"A lot of guys." I suck back the tears but more continue to cascade down my cheeks. "My boyfriend, the one I had when the accident happened, said he couldn't handle it, that my life was too complicated for him. That I'd ruin his life if I stayed with him."

"He said that to you?" Jax asks, and I nod. "What a fucking asshole." He grinds his teeth. "I can't believe he said that to you. I want to hit him."

"He was just being honest. And it was better for him to bail out early than leave later on." I dab my eyes with the bottom of my shirt.

He studies me closely then relaxes, as if suddenly something is making sense. "I want to be part of your complicated life, just as long as you want me to be." He says it so simply, so matter-of-factly.

"Jax, you don't get it. Things are really hard—"

162

He covers his hand over my mouth. "I understand you have a lot of stuff going on, but I hope you'll make room for me. Because I don't want this," he removes his hand and gestures between us, "to end. I'm happy. You make me happy even when I'm back here, which may not seem like a whole lot, but it's a really huge deal."

"I don't know what to say." I expected him to flip out and now that he hasn't, I don't know what to do with myself.

"Don't say anything right now. Just think about it for a while." He slides back toward the headboard and stretches his legs out. "Go take a shower and I'll go get the snacks. I think I'll try to find a little more information on Marcus, but if we haven't found any information by Saturday morning, we're going to have to take off. We need to have time for you to go up to the Tetons on our way home."

"We don't have to do that if there's not time." I scoot to the edge of the bed and lower my feet onto the floor. "We should spend all the time we need looking for your mom. That's what the trip is for."

"Just stop. We're going to scatter your father's ashes and you're going to get to say your goodbye. I'll even hold your hand the entire time."

"Wow, I feel so honored." I manage to crack a small joke.

"There's my girl," he says with pride.

My heart leaps in my chest. After telling him what I just did, I'm surprised it can still beat at all. After Mack, it broke, but somehow, Jax has made it feel more whole.

Chapter Eleven

Jax

We spend most of the next day asking about my mother and Marcus around town. The problem is most of the people who know them aren't the most reliable sources.

"I feel like I'm on crackhead/prostitute overload." A shiver courses through Clara's body as we sit in the car, eating ice cream and taking a much needed break from our search.

"I completely agree." I suck the vanilla ice cream off the spoon, noting from my peripheral vision that Clara is observing my every movement.

"Want to tell me what's on your mind?" I ask, scooping up another spoonful of vanilla goodness.

She shrugs with her eyes still glued on me. "I was just thinking… about us."

"How did you go from talking about crackheads and prostitutes to us?"

"I don't know. I think I've been thinking about us the entire day. My head's only really been half into finding your mom."

"I wish mine was." I set down the cup of ice cream and lay my arm on the back of her seat. "So, what exactly are you thinking about?"

She shrugs, stuffing her mouth with a bite of chocolate ice cream. "I was just wondering how things were going to go when we got back home."

I tangle my fingers through her hair and try not to smile when she doesn't pull away. After she opened up to me last night, she seems to be a bit more affectionate. "That's really up to you. I've always been pretty clear on what I want."

"But you still want that?" She seems so positive I've somehow changed my mind about wanting her, just because she told me about her family.

I still can't believe she was so worried over telling me about her mother. That she thought I'd leave her like her ex-boyfriend did. Seriously, what a fucking asshole. Clearly, he's never experienced the pain of life before.

"Of course I do." I resist an eye roll at her silliness. "I should probably tell you something, though. Something you might freak out over."

She stirs her ice cream with the spoon, growing anxious. "Okay."

I cross my fingers she doesn't freak out, but I feel like I need to tell her.

"I'm going to be living really close to you soon," I divulge then hold my breath and wait for her response.

"How close?"

"Right next door close."

Her brows dip. "You mean…"

"I mean, I rented a place in your apartment complex. The place right next door to yours, actually."

Her lips part but no sound comes out. She shovels up a spoonful of ice cream and stuffs it into her mouth.

"Are you okay?" I slip my fingers from her hair to the back of her neck and trace circles on her skin.

"I'm fine. I just… you've looked at the place, right? I mean, they're not nice apartments."

"You've seen where I grew up, right?" I remind her. "And yes, I have looked at the places. They look fine to me. Cheap but livable. And affordable, which is the best part."

"And right next to where I live." She doesn't sound as upset as I expected her to be.

"Another added bonus."

She absentmindedly stirs her ice cream. "When do you move in?"

"A few weeks after we get back." I move my hand away from her neck to pick up my ice cream cup. "Are you going to be okay with that?"

She shrugs, licking a drop of ice cream off the spoon. "What would you do if I said I wasn't?" She locks gazes with me. "Would you not move there?"

I feel like I'm walking into a trap. "I don't know… probably not. There's no place else I can afford, and I'm really ready to move out of Avery's."

She considers what I've said. "Well, if you need to live there then you need to live there."

"So, you're okay with me being so close?"

"I'm sure having you so close will have some perks."

"Are you being dirty right now?" I question.

"Maybe," she replies vaguely.

I smile and relax, feeling a weight lift off my chest. But the pressure builds right back up when I spot one of my mother's old friends, Melinda, ducking behind the ice cream shop.

"Wait here. I see someone my mom knows," I tell Clara then scramble out of the car and chase after Melinda.

I hurry around the back of the building and find her leaning against the back door, smoking a joint right out in the open.

"Hey, baby." She grins when she sees me then adjusts her boobs in her neon pink top. "You looking for a good time?"

"Melinda, it's me, Jax." When she doesn't seem to recognize me I add, "Jax Hensley."

"Jax." She smiles genuinely this time as she stands up straight. "Holy shit. How the hell have you been?"

"Good." I hold my breath as she moves in for a hug and only breathe again when she steps away.

"What have you been up to?" She pinches the joint between her fingers. "I heard you moved to North Carolina or some shit."

"Yeah, I'm going to school. So's Avery."

"Good. It's so good you two got out." She glances at the street at a group of people I'm fairly certain are dealing drugs. "Not a lot of people do."

"Yeah, I know." I scratch at the back of my neck. "Look, have you by chance seen my mom around? I've been meaning to talk to her."

She suddenly grows twitchy, scratching her scabbed arms and biting on her dry lips. "Oh honey, I don't think so... Is that why you're here? Are you looking for her?" I nod, and she shakes her head. "Do yourself a favor and go home."

"I can't until I find her. The last I heard, she was working for this Marcus guy."

"Go home, Jax." She backs toward the group on the corner of the street. "You'll regret it if you don't."

I'm not sure if it's a threat or not, but I'm annoyed because I'm pretty certain she probably knows where my mother is and isn't telling me.

By the time I climb back in the car, I'm stewing in irritation. Another dead end. Another person who doesn't want to tell me anything.

"I'm guessing that didn't go very well," Clara says when she catches a glimpse of my face.

I shake my head and rev up the engine. "Nope. This place is driving me crazy."

"You look like maybe you could use a nap." Clara collects a napkin from the glove box and cleans the sticky ice cream off her fingers. "You even have dark circles under your eyes." She balls the napkin up and stuffs it in the cup holder.

"Is that your not so subtle way of telling me I look like shit?" I twist around in the seat to look out the rear window while I back out of the parking space.

"No, that was my unsubtle way of saying maybe we should go back to the motel and get some rest. It's been a long day." She checks her messages on her phone, something I've noticed she does a lot. Maybe because she worries about her mother.

I tap on the brakes and shift into first gear. "It's only five o'clock, though. We still have a lot of daylight left."

"How about this." She tugs an elastic band out of her hair and runs her finger through the braid. "We go back for like an hour and take a nap? Then we can come back out. The sun will still be up." She peers up at the crystal blue sky. "The sun stays up freakishly late here."

"Only in the summer." The tires skid as I pull out onto the street. "In the winter, it seems dark twenty-four-seven—" My foot slams down on the brakes as a man skitters out into the road. "Holy fucking shit." I breathe with wide eyes as we miss hitting him by an inch.

The man is dressed in rags, his shoes have holes in the soles, and his overly long beard and hair are matted with dirt and God knows what else.

Instead of hurrying out of the street, he rounds to the driver side of the Jeep and raps on the window. "Hey, can you spare some change? I'm in a real bad place, man, and I'd greatly appreciate it."

A beat skips by as I slowly realize who the man hidden underneath the beard and baggy clothes is.

"Lester?" My hands stiffen on the wheel at the sight of the man who was one of the main causes for me moving to North Carolina. He was my mother's husband at the time. He'd tried to beat my mother one night for no reason other than he was trippin' balls. When I'd stepped in, he'd come at me swinging, and I'd swung back.

"Who's Lester?" Clara hisses under her breath. "That name sounds familiar."

"The man I got into the fight with… the one I told you about."

Her lips form an *O*. "Maybe we should just go."

We probably should, but Lester did a lot of messed up shit to me when I was younger and I couldn't defend myself. Seeing him now, at such a low point in his life, I want to witness his suffering for a little longer. That might make me a really shitty person, but I can't help how I feel. The man caused me a lot of pain, broken bones, bruises. He had this thing with beating me with a belt too, which not only hurt but was humiliating since I was fifteen years old. He also mentally fucked me up, always telling me what a useless piece of shit I was.

Lester tilts his head to the side as he studies me through the glass. "Jax Hensley?" He lets out a nervous laugh, itching at the backs of his hands. "I thought you moved or some shit."

"I did," I reply tightly. "I'm just looking for my mother. Have you seen her?" I hate asking him—hate him—but he might know where she is.

His eyelids lower as he stares at me. "That all depends."

I resist an eye roll. "How much do you want?"

He leans up to the window and fogs up the glass with his breathing. "How much you got?"

"Not a lot."

"How about fifty bucks."

I shake my head. "Twenty."

"Twenty-five." He makes a grabby hand. "Yeah, twenty-five will get me a lot."

I remove my wallet from my pocket and grab twenty-five dollars.

"Are you sure you want to do that?" Clara whispers so Lester won't hear her. "He doesn't look very reliable."

"Yeah, but the two of them hang out with the same crowd so he could know where she is." I roll the window down, and the stench of garbage mixed with smoke and booze whisks inside the cab. I'm fairly positive he is the culprit of the stench.

"Thanks, Jax." He steals the money from my hands, his bloodshot eyes lighting up like a kid opening presents on Christmas morning.

"Tell me what you know, or I'll take it back," I warn, pulling the emergency brake.

He stuffs the cash into the pocket of his oversized coat then glances up and down the road before shuffling closer. "The last I heard, she was with that Marcus guy everyone's been talking about."

"Yeah, so I've heard."

He lowers his voice. "He's not someone you want to piss off, you know."

"And my mother pissed him off."

His shifty gaze darts to a car driving by in the lane next to us. "You know how your mother gets. She's always thinking about herself. That kind of attitude is what gets people into trouble with big shots like Marcus." He rests his arms on the windowsill and leans in. "He even has his own bodyguards and everything."

I trap my breath in my lungs as the stench of him stings my nostrils. "Do you know where I can find this Marcus?"

"If I did, I wouldn't tell you," he says. "You don't want to mess around with him."

"Let's not stand here and pretend you actually give as shit about me." I flex my fingers as my jaw ticks. "How much more do you want?"

His eyes drift to the sky as he considers it. "Fifteen."

"Ten."

"Twelve."

Shaking my head, I snatch a ten and two ones from my wallet, and chuck the money at him. "Now where can I find this Marcus?" I ask Lester as he scrambles to collect the money as it gets blown away by the wind.

"There's a club called Neon Madness. It's down in the main center of town." He catches the bills in his greedy little hands. "Go tomorrow, though. He's more likely to show up on a Friday night."

"Neon Madness," I mutter under my breath as I roll the window back up. Then I unlock the emergency brake, press on the gas, and drive forward. "That must be a new place."

"You think he was telling the truth?" Clara asks, side braiding her hair. "He seemed kind of shady."

"He seemed like a meth head, which is what he is."

"Hey, are you okay? I mean, it had to be hard seeing him."

"I'm fine," I lie then sigh exhaustedly. "I'm just ready to go home. That's all."

"Is there anything I can do to help?" She ties a band around her hair, securing the braid in place.

"I can think of a few things you can do when we get back to the room that might cheer me up." I wiggle my brows suggestively.

But truth is, after seeing Lester—after being reminded of my past and the pain he caused me—I'd rather her just hold me.

Chapter Twelve

Clara

Jax looks so sad after talking to Lester, and I want nothing more than to make him feel better. After I told him about my mother and my life, he was so understanding and made me feel at ease. I need to return the favor, which is exactly what I do when we get back to the motel.

"I was thinking we could eat at this restaurant tonight," Jax says, shutting the motel room door. "It's not fancy or anything, but I'm getting burnt out on hamburgers and fries."

I drop my purse on a table near the window. "Me too."

"So it's a date then." He skims the screen of his phone before setting it down on the nightstand. Then he removes the ring from his finger and the wallet from his pocket and places them beside the phone.

"It can be a date on one condition." I sink into a chair and slump back, worn out. While there have been good times on this trip, it's also been mentally draining.

I almost can't wait to get home, back to my crazy world. I miss my mom. Nelli. I miss the warmth of my home. Funny, it took leaving and seeing such an ugly side of life to appreciate my world.

"Bargaining time." Jax lies down on the mattress and stretches out his arms. His shirt rides up, and I get an eyeful of the lean muscles carving his stomach. "My favorite time of the day."

"Mine too," I agree distractedly, gawking at him like he's delicious candy I want to take a bite out of.

"Are you enjoying yourself?" he asks haughtily, raising the hem of his shirt higher.

I could try to pretend I wasn't just eye fucking his body, but at this point the effort would be worthless. I'm pretty much drooling.

"So, the bargain." I artlessly change the subject, leaning over to unbuckle my sandals. "I'll go to the restaurant with you and even let you call it a date, just as long as you'll let me pay for dinner."

"Fuck no. I'm too much of a gentlemen to let you do that," he says, offended. When I give him a *really* look, he rolls over onto his stomach. "Are you saying I'm not a gentleman?"

I wiggle my foot out of the sandal then move to unbuckle the other. "A gentleman would never say ninety percent of the stuff that comes out of your mouth."

His jaw drops, and he mockingly places his hand over his mouth. "I can't believe you just said that to me. After all the door opening I've done for you. I even let you violate me when you insisted you had to be the boss. Some of the stuff you did made me feel so dirty."

I stare blankly at him, racking my brain for a comeback. Laughter overcomes me, though, and my head falls forward as I bust up laughing. "Sometimes… I can't even…" After the hilarity settles, I wipe the happy tears from my eyes and raise my head back up. He's grinning at me from the bed, totally pleased with himself. "Gentleman or not, I still want to pay for dinner." After him forking out money to Lester, it's the least I can do.

"I don't want you to do that." He straightens his arms, pushes up from the bed, and sits up. "I know you're struggling financially."

"We both are," I remind him, slipping my foot out of my sandal.

"Yeah, but," he hesitates, "you have your mom to take care of."

179

"I know I do." It's strange talking about my mother with him. It's been so long since I've discussed her situation with anyone besides Nelli. "But let me just pay this one time." I rise from the chair and move toward the bed. "You've paid for pretty much everything on this trip." I slide my knees onto the bed and kneel in front of him, wanting to tear his clothes off.

His hands find my waist, and he pulls me onto his lap. "You have a very unlady-like look in your eyes right now."

I clasp onto his shoulders. "So what? I never claimed to be a lady."

"I know. I'm glad you're not. I'm too naughty to be with a lady."

A quiet giggle escapes my lips. It's been a long time since I've been this relaxed and at ease.

"You want to keep going with the mouth foreplay? Or just give in and kiss me like you've wanted to all day?" he challenges. His hands skate underneath my dress, and he grips my ass.

Cocky little bastard.

"I agreed to cheer you up." I lick my lips. "So I'm going to cheer you up." Without any warning, I shove him back. He lands with a grunt, but I give him no time to recover as I grab the bottom of his shirt and yank it over his head. Then I drag my fingers down his chest, just rough enough to leave faint red lines on his flesh.

"Clara," he begins to protest as I flick open the button of his jeans. Over what, I don't know and I don't care.

I've always been comfortable in bed with Jax, and taking charge never was a problem. Sure, I blush here and there. In fact, my cheeks are heated right now as my fingers delve below his boxers, but I never get embarrassed enough to stop.

Jax watches me with inquisitiveness written all over his face as I wrap my fingers around his swollen cock.

"Why are you looking at me like that?" I ask as my thumb skims over the tip of him.

He inhales a sharp breath through his nose and pleasure ripples through his body. "I'm just…" he struggles for words. "Trying to figure out what's… going on inside… your head." His neck arches as his head tips back against the pillow. "I find you…" He stops talking as I move my hand up and down.

I shift to the side and let go of his cock, only to tug his jeans lower. Then I return my hand to him and continue to slide my fingers up and down while watching him lose control. Finally, when he looks on the verge of losing it, I dip my head and take him in my mouth like I did the first night we hooked up.

I don't even know why I did it the first time. Oral sex wasn't something Mack and I explored. But I was buzzed and horny and curious, and Jax pretty much let me do whatever I wanted to him. It made me feel kind of powerful in a life I had no power over.

A throaty groan escapes his mouth, and I peer up at him through my eyelashes. His Adam's apple bobs up and down as he swallows hard and rakes his fingers through his hair. Moments later, he utters my name and reaches down toward me. Cupping my cheeks, he moves my mouth off him right before his body jerks, and he comes apart. After he finishes and cleans himself up, he pulls up his jeans, reclines against the headboard, and opens his arms.

"Come here." His brows are dipped in confusion.

I hesitate at his request. Holding me is so intimate. Something we've never done before. But when his expression starts to plummet, I scoot up to him and rest my head against his chest with my ear right over his heart.

His pulse is jackhammering, and his skin has a light sheen of sweat, but the warmth of his flesh settles my reservations about cuddling.

"You didn't have to do that." He drapes an arm over my back and soothingly smoothes his free hand across the back of my head.

"I know. I wanted to." My eyelids shut as sleep overtakes me.

And that's how we end up dozing off—in each other's arms with our bodies tangled together. I have no clue where he starts and I end.

Maybe we start and end together.

Chapter Thirteen

Clara

About an hour later, I wake up from my nap. My head is resting on Jax's chest and my hand is on his bare stomach.

I push up and glance at the time. "Man, it's late," I mutter, rubbing my eyes.

Out the window, the moon illuminates from the dark sky and headlights dot the street. Now that it's nighttime, the sleepy little town has woken up.

"Hey you," Jax says groggily as he slowly wakes up from dreamland. He looks at the alarm clock on the nightstand. "How long have you been awake?"

"Only a couple of minutes." My belly lets out the hungriest grumble ever.

His eyes crinkle around the corners as he laughs. "A little bit hungry, are you?"

My cheeks redden as I nod. "Apparently so."

He sits up on the bed, kicking the sheet off him. "Let's go feed that bad boy then."

He changes into a clean shirt while I quickly fix my makeup and put my sandals back on. Then we head out of the room, get into the car, and drive toward the opposite side of town.

"It's like everyone was sleeping during the day," I comment as I watch a seemingly endless amount of cars and trucks zip up and down the street. "I'm starting to wonder if the whole vampire thing wasn't a joke."

"It'd probably be better if it wasn't," he says bitterly. "The truth is worse."

"What's the truth?"

"That everyone's waking up to get high, drunk, sell drugs, sell themselves. You name the illegal activity and it's probably happening right now."

Just then, I spot a few women and men passing around a joint on a street corner. By the time we arrive at the restaurant, I've seen two fights, a hooker get into a car, and a man scale a tree like a monkey, which according to Jax is probably because the man's trippin' balls.

"We can go back to the hotel if you want," he says to me after the car is parked. "I know being out this late in this town is a lot to take in."

The restaurant doesn't look so terrible. The building structure is stable and freshly painted. Little twinkly lights sparkle in the windows and tulips line the pathway to the entrance door.

"No, I'm good. This place actually looks nice." I smile, hoping to ease his worries.

He relaxes a smidgeon but tenses the moment we get out of the car. When we reach the front of the Jeep, he snatches my hand and clutches on tightly.

"Everything okay?" I ask as we cross the mostly vacant parking lot.

He edgily peers at the vehicles around us. "Yeah, I'm just thinking about when I came here with my mom. "

That doesn't really explain his strange behavior.

"But why do you seem so nervous?" I ask as he opens the door for me. I step inside, and the warm, delicious smell of chicken and biscuits engulfs me.

"Because we weren't here to eat." He moves up to the hostess desk and tells her a table for two. After she wanders off to go check for available tables, Jax inches closer to me and lowers his voice. "I was about five-years-old. She came here to meet a client of hers. Usually she'd just do her thing in the car, but this time the guy wanted to go to a motel. So she piled me and Avery in this creepy asshole's car." His

186

eyes glaze over as he stares off at the tables. "The thing I remember the most is that it smelled like peanuts and fish, but that's probably because Avery and I had to sit in the damn car for three hours while the two of them went into the room. It was winter and really fucking cold—they didn't even leave the heater on. I kept saying I was cold and begged Avery to go get our mom. She was too afraid to go get her, though, so instead she just hugged me until they finally came out." His brows dip, and then he shakes his head. "I'm sorry. That was totally an inappropriate story for our first date."

"No, you're fine." I suck back the tears, step in front of him, and catch his gaze. "I think you and I have reached beyond the point of inappropriate stories. We've told each other so much already." The realization of my words strike me deeply, but not in a negative way. "And this is techni-cally our first date, but not really."

A hint of a smile rises on his lips. "So, what you're saying is our friends with benefits thing was just an excuse? That really the whole time, you were secretly dating me?"

"You're making it sound like it was a one-sided thing," I muse. "Like it was all me."

"You know that's not true." His lips dip to my ear, and my shoulder judders. "I think you've known for a really long time that I've wanted us to be together. That I was just playing along with you until you realized how much you liked me." He nips my earlobe, causing my skin to flush with heat.

"Maybe…" I trail off as the hostess wanders up to us with a cheery smile on her face.

"Right this way." She motions us to follow her then leads the way to a corner booth.

Instead of sitting across from me, Jax slides into the seat beside me. The hostess places menus on the table in front of us and starts filling up our glasses with water.

"You're really going to sit there?" I ask Jax, opening the menu.

The hostess gives me a strange look, as if she can't fathom why I'd ask Jax that question.

"I like being close to you." He flashes the hostess a charismatic grin. "She secretly likes that I'm sitting by her. She just doesn't want to admit it."

The woman giggles and damn near swoons to the floor. "Your waitress will be over in just a few." She smiles at Jax then blasts me with a death glare before whisking away to the front of the restaurant.

"Wow, it's like a gift," I remark, skimming over the drinks.

"What is?

"The way you charm people."

A questioning look crosses his face. "Who did I just charm?"

I elevate my brows. "Are you joking right now?"

He shakes his head, looking utterly lost. "Nope."

I scoot closer to him and lower my voice. "The hostess. She just about fainted just from you smiling at her." I discretely point toward the front of the restaurant. "And she hasn't been able to stop staring at us since."

He gives a blasé glance at the front desk then locks his attention back on me. "Are you jealous?"

I shake my head. "No way."

"Why not?" He juts out his bottom lip, pouting sexily.

"You really want me to be one of those girl's that gets jealous simply because her boyfriend smiles at another girl..." My eyes widen as I realize what I just said. My gaze dashes back to the menu and I clear my throat, desperately seeking a subject change. "So, what's good here?" I casually ask as I scan over the list of items on the menu.

A beat or two goes by. The sound of clinking glasses and chatter fill the uncomfortable silence between us. I wonder what he's thinking. I wonder what the hell I was thinking dropping the b word like that. *Boyfriend.* Jax isn't my boyfriend. Although it kind of seemed like he offered to play the role after I poured my heart and soul out to him.

"I'm not sure." He breaks the silence but then pauses again. I peek at him from the corner of my eye. His head is tilted to the side, his eyes on the list of appetizers. "I've only eaten here once. On my ninth birthday."

Relief washes over me at the subject change. "Who'd you come here with?"

"Avery." He flips the page of the menu. "We had to ransack the house for change and ride the bus for an hour just to get to this place, but it was probably the best birthday I ever had while I was living here. She even bought me a slice of pie, which was the closest thing to a birthday cake I've ever had." A trace of a smile appears on his lips. "Avery was always good with taking care of me. It's why I've always been so happy to help her out with Mason."

I tuck my leg under me and rotate sideways in the booth, facing him. "Is she going to be okay when you move out?"

"She has Tristan now."

"That's her boyfriend, right? The one who was in the hospital?" I've briefly met Avery, Tristan, and even Mason because I was on call when they came into the emergency room.

"Yeah, he was protecting her from her ex-husband." He picks up his cup of ice water and takes a sip. "As bad as this is going to sound, I'm glad the fight happened between the two of them because it got her douche bag of an ex-husband into jail where he belongs."

I didn't know Jax very well back then, but he's told me enough about his life that I know Avery's ex-husband is in jail for assault and drug possession.

The story hits a halt as the waitress comes to take our orders, and collect our menus. When she leaves, Jax shakes his head.

"Wow, I'm turning into the worst date ever, sitting here telling you all my depressing stories," he mutters. "I don't know what my problem is, but I feel way off my game."

"You're fine." I unroll the napkin that's around the silverware. "And it has to be hard being here and remembering everything."

"No, that's not it. You're making me nervous."

"Why? What did I do?"

"You keep saying things that give me hope."

"I'm sorry." I have no idea what else to say.

"Don't be sorry. I like it. I just need to get my swagger back."

A giggle erupts from my lips and he grins along with me. But seconds later, the smile evaporates and a determined look emerges on his face.

He turns toward me and brings his knee up onto the booth so that it's touching mine. "Tell me something happy."

I'm thrown by the sudden demand. "Like what?"

He shrugs. "I don't know. How about a story about your childhood?"

I can't help but smile. "There's so many stories I don't even know where to start."

"Tell me about your ninth birthday," he suggests, stirring his straw around in his water.

"My ninth birthday." I pick at the corners of the napkin. "I think that was the birthday my father took me to the beach. We spent the entire day collecting seashells. We were supposed to stay until sundown, but we had to go home early after I decided I was going to run out into the ocean to catch the magic out of a wave and almost ended up drowning."

Ruin Me

"*What*? You almost drown because you wanted to catch the magic out of the wave?"

"Well, on top of having a ridiculously overactive imagination, I also couldn't swim. But I was the kind of kid who didn't show a lot of fear. In fact, I think for a while I actually believed I was immortal."

"You were okay, though, right?" he asks then shakes his head. "Well, clearly you are since you're here."

"My father came in after me about two seconds after I barreled in there. He pulled me out, wrapped me in a towel, and yelled at me." I softly laugh as I remember how angry he looked then how guilty he was ten seconds later. "By the time we made it to the car, he was apologizing left and right. He felt so bad for yelling at me, even though he had every right to."

"He sounds like he was a good dad."

"He was." My voice is uneven and my eyes burn with tears as I recollect all the great times I had with my dad up until he died. I suck in deep breaths of air, trying to keep the waterworks back.

He delicately cups my cheek. "You know what I think we should do?"

193

"What?" A tear manages to escape and rolls down my cheek.

"I think for your next birthday we should go to the beach and catch magic in the waves all day. You can swim now, right?"

Laughing, I wipe the tear away with the back of my hand. "Yes, I can swim now. Although, I still never have figured out how to catch magic in the waves."

"We'll figure it out," he promises. "Just as long as you promise to let me spend your next birthday with you."

He's asking me for way more than just a birthday. He knows it. I know it. Part of me wants to bolt out of the booth. But after spending so much time with Jax, learning who he is, and opening up to him, I'm starting to wonder if he'll protect my heart for me.

"I'll tell you what." My voice is still a little unsteady, but for an entirely different reason. "You can spend my next birthday with me catching magic in the waves if I can spend your next birthday with you, baking you an absurdly awesome cake."

His brow crooks. "You can bake?"

"Kind of. My Aunt Nelli's really good at it, so I can get some pointers from her." I playfully bump my shoulder into his. "Don't worry. I promise you'll have an amazing day."

"I believe you."

"Good. So is it a deal?"

"It's a deal." His tongue slides out and wets his lips. "I want to kiss you right now." He doesn't lean in and take the kiss. He waits for me to offer it.

I nod my head once and the movement is easier than I thought it would be.

He frees a breath then moves in and touches his lips to mine. The kiss is quick, just a soft caress of lips, a teasing taste, just enough to leave me craving more.

More kisses.

More touches.

More of him.

Chapter Fourteen

Jax

After we leave the restaurant, we return to the motel and spend the next hour kissing until we fall asleep in bed. In the early hours of daybreak, we wake up, get dressed, and hit the streets to ask around for my mother. But everyone seems about as hesitant as Melinda to divulge anything.

The day is exhausting, but Clara is a trooper. With each passing hour, I become more grateful she's here with me, not just because she's opening up to me more but because she's been really good at keeping me together. Every time I grow frustrated, she calms me down and forces me to take a break. I think I might be falling in love with her and wish I could get the courage to tell her how I feel, but the time doesn't seem right.

Still, now that I know more about her, maybe our relationship can move forward now—that the whole friends with benefits deal can come to an end. While she did make the promise to spend our next birthdays together, she still hasn't verbally revoked her friends-with-benefits rules, so all I can do is wait until she decides if she trusts me—if she wants me as more than a fuck buddy.

196

Around eight o'clock at night, I peel out of the gas station and cruise toward Neon Madness to see if by chance Marcus has shown up. I'm a little nervous about going straight to the source, but at this point I don't see another option.

On our way there, Clara and I stop at a fast food place to grab a quick bite to eat. The inside of the car stinks like grease and fries, and our shakes are melting in the cup holders.

"What do you think the odds are that Lester told the truth about Marcus being at this place?" Clara asks as she pops a fry into her mouth.

"He's about as reliable as everyone else we've talked to, so the odds seem kind of low." I slow at a stop sign and steal a fry from the bag on Clara's lap. "But, at this point, I have to try any lead I can get."

I crank up the heater. With the clouds rolling in, the air is even breezier than it normally is in May. That's the thing about Wyoming—summer, fall, winter, spring, the nights are always cold.

"So, this club that we're going to, is it like the Dirty Tiger?" Clara picks up a cup of Coke and takes a sip from the straw.

"I honestly don't know. I've never heard of it until yesterday." I flip on the headlights as the sun descends below the mountains, and night progressively shadows the land.

"I hope not." She dunks a fry into a cup of ranch. "That place was so gross. And I don't care if that makes me sound sheltered. I'm starting to realize being sheltered might not be a bad thing."

"No, it's definitely not," I agree, making a right at the next intersection.

We drive up the main street bordered by bars, diners, and knickknack stores until Neon Madness comes into view. Every square foot of the building has been spray-painted with florescent hues of green, pink, yellow, and orange. Lights of similar colors flash vibrantly from through the windows and along the trim of the room.

"Well, the name is fitting," I remark as I flip on my blinker to turn into the gravelly parking lot.

"It doesn't look as bad as the Dirty Tiger." Clara sits forward in the seat as she examines the place.

"We still should be careful." I silence the engine and slide the keys out of the ignition. "If my mom hangs out here, I'm betting this place is a lot sketchier than it looks."

Clara nods anxiously as she unbuckles her seatbelt. "Got it."

We open our doors to get out, and I stuff my keys into my pocket as I move up beside her. When I swing my arm over her shoulders protectively, she doesn't inch away like she would have a few days ago. After opening up to me, she's been way more affectionate.

"What are you thinking about?" Clara asks.

I shrug. "Just how beautiful you are."

Completely true. With the short red dress, strappy sandals that wrap up her long, lean legs, and her hair pulled up, she's going to turn heads the moment we step into the club.

"You've been so serious today," she muses as we approach the front door where a hefty guy I assume is the bouncer is eyeballing us. "Are you okay?"

"What do you mean by serious?"

Her sandals scuff against the gravel. "I don't know. You just haven't cracked a lot of jokes or made any dirty remarks about how short my dress is yet."

"Is someone missing my perviness?" I tease and she doesn't deny it. "I was just giving you some space while you thought about stuff, but since you brought it up..." I reach up the back of her dress and pinch her ass, eliciting a squeal from her.

She fights back a grin as she skitters out from under my arm. "I didn't mean for you to start right back up."

"You know what, I think you did want me to start up." I charm her with a grin. "I think that, deep down, you really, really like my dirty mouth."

She crosses her arms and raises her brows. "So what if I do?"

"So, you're admitting you like me?" I try not to grin but fail epically.

"Well, I think it's pretty obvious I like you." Her eyes roam to my dick.

I bite my lip to keep from laughing at her. Then I snatch hold of her hips and reel her against me. "But you like me, like me."

With a quivering breath, she bobs her head up and down. "I do."

I close my eyes and breathe in the cool air. Despite where we are and why we're here, I want to enjoy this moment. "Do you want to skip going to this place and go back to the motel for a little bit?"

"But it's not Friday."

My eyes shoot open. "Seriously? After what you did to me last night you're going to go back to that?"

"I'm just kidding." She laughs maliciously. "Besides, it is Friday, silly."

"Oh, yeah." Through all the stress, I'd somehow forgotten. An artful smirk curves at my lips. "Guess tonight is bow-chicka-bow-wow night, huh?"

"I guess so." She suddenly grows serious as she warily looks over at the club. "I do think we should finish up with this, though. Maybe we'll luck out and find your mom and then we can enjoy the rest of the night." She gives my hand a squeeze.

"Yeah, maybe." I'm more skeptical of the outcome, though. Even if by some miracle Marcus is here and he easily tells us my mother is alive and where she is, actually seeing her will more than likely ruin my night.

But knowing I'll only have peace of mind when I know she's not dead, I hold onto Clara's hand and we walk up to the bouncer. He asks to check our ID's. Since I don't have a fake one, I give him my real one, hoping he'll glance over it and let me through. Surprisingly, he does just that. The moment we enter the club, I quickly discover the reason for his carelessness. Half the people packed inside the small room are my age, if not younger.

"It's dark in here," Clara shouts over the bass of the music, the neon green lighting reflecting in her eyes.

I nod, intensifying my hold on her hand. I squeeze by people dancing and grinding on one another to the sultry rhythm of a song, leading Clara with me. When we reach an area where the crowd thins, I take a good look around and realize there isn't a bar anywhere.

Odd.

Most of the crowd has paint on their skin that matches the shades on the exterior of the building. The paint glows against the black lights on the steel ceiling beams, and glitter is falling from somewhere. Almost every single person looks possessed by sheer lust, dry humping and fondling one another.

"It's like an orgy!" Clara says with wide eyes as she watches the scene in front of us.

"Yeah, I think you got your rave wish!' I holler over the electric music as we get jostled and groped by people.

"What do you mean?" She squints at the sweaty mob swarming us. "Wait, are they…"

I nod then offer her an apologetic look. "Leave it to my mother to be in a place filled with people rolling."

"Are we going to be okay here?" She gapes at two people in the corner who are one step away from peeling each other's clothes off and fucking right in front of us.

I cover her eyes and inch her toward a quieter spot in the room where people seem a little less handsy.

She tugs my hand away from her eyes. "Jax, I've seen people have sex before."

My brow shoots up. "When?"

She raises a shoulder and gives a laidback shrug. "In porn movies."

My jaw just about smacks the floor. "You watch porn?"

"I have a couple of times when I was hanging out with Mack and his friends..." She floats away in a memory then promptly shakes her head. "Where do you think I get all those dirty ideas from?"

I pull her toward me until our hips flush. "Clara McKiney, you've been holding out an important details about you."

"Give me time." Her eyes blue look teal vibrant neon green lights. "You'll get to know all my little quirks."

"I'm looking forward to it." I roll my hips into hers, totally turned on by what she divulged.

"I'm learning stuff about you, too."

She doesn't object when I reach around and sneak my hand up the bottom of her dress. "And what's that?"

"That you're horny all the time."

"I think you already knew that…" My grin falters when I notice a taller man wearing a suit enter the club. A hush falls over the crowd as everyone gawks at him.

"Who is that?" I ask a guy dancing pretty close to us.

"That's Marcus Dalemaring." The guy turns to me, he scans me over, and then a grin curls his painted lips. "You looking for a good time, sexy?"

"Um…" I look to Clara for help, but she only giggles, enjoying my discomfort.

"A shy one, huh?" He prowls toward me and jives his hips in my direction.

I dodge around Clara, snag her arm, and tow her to the edge of the crowd.

"That was freaking hilarious." Clara laughs harder, gasping for air. "I've never seen you so uncomfortable before."

"The dude dry humped me."

She catches her breath as her laughter dwindles. "Hey, I thought it was kind of hot."

I blink at her. "What?"

"Oh, this is going to be fun." She rubs her hands together with a wicked glint in her eyes.

"What's going to be fun?" My gaze is trained on Marcus as he saunters through the crowd with two very large and bulky guys at his side. Well, more like the crowd parts for all three of them.

"Paying you back for all those times you teased me." She pinches my ass, and I flinch, but keep my eyes on Marcus.

"Who is that?" Clara wonders as she tracks my gaze

"The guy back there said it's Marcus." I rush toward him as Marcus strides toward a door located along the back wall of the club. "Wait here," I call over my shoulder to Clara.

"Jax!" she protests, but when I shoot her a warning look over my shoulder, she nods and stays put.

Good. The last thing I need is for her to get further into this mess.

I square my shoulders and march my way up to the man who may have killed my mother. The only calming factor in the situation is that we're in a room full of people, so he can't do anything to me if he has some vengeance plan against my mother.

"Hey, Marcus," I holler as I approach him, elbowing a guy out of my way.

The two big guys who walked in with Marcus immediately step together and block him from my view.

"Back off, kid," one of them warns, shoving me back.

My back slams into a girl who instantly starts griping about my clumsiness. I brush her off though, my attention fixed on Marcus.

"Relax, I just need to ask him a question." I lean to the side but the guy just sidesteps. "Seriously, I just need to know if he's seen my mother."

Marcus appears at the big dude's side, looking very interested in my question. "I thought you looked familiar. You must be Jax Hensley."

What the fuck?

"Yeah, but how do you know that?" I cross my arms and stare him down, despite how uneasy I feel.

"I've seen pictures of you." He carries my stare with such a manner of confidence. I grow even more anxious. This man clearly doesn't worry about much. "Well, a picture. She likes to show it to people all the time. Her son. Her pride and joy."

I shake my head. "That's a lie. My mother doesn't give a shit about me."

His expression darkens. "Okay, I might have embellished the last part, but she does have a picture of you in her house."

In my house? So he's been there. He was probably the one who broke the door down too.

I clench my hands into fists, my nails piercing my palms. "Do you know where my mother is?" I ask through gritted teeth.

A smirk rises on his face. "I haven't seen her since," a thoughtful look crosses his expression, "since about four days ago when she begged for her life and promised she'd pay me back my thousand dollars."

I inch toward him, ignoring the big guy's warning to stay back. "What did you do to her?"

"I didn't do anything to her." His voice is like ice as he leans in to my face. "But if you do see her, tell her I'm still waiting for my money. And I'm not a very patient man." With that, he turns and heads toward the back door.

I try to follow after him, but one of his bodyguards pushes me back so forcefully I stumble into a wall.

"Fuck!" I curse, kicking the wall.

A few people glance in my direction, but they're too high to question what my problem is. I tug at my hair, wanting to scream. Why the fuck does my mother have to get herself into this shit? Why do I have to care so damn much?

Through my fit of rage, warm fingers envelop my arm. I don't have to look up to know the hand belongs to Clara. I allow her to guide me out of the club and across the parking lot. By the time we reach the car, I'm so damn frustrated I'm shaking.

"Give me your keys," she demands, sticking out her hand.

I hand them over without arguing, knowing I'm too riled up to be behind the wheel.

We get in the car, and she drives out onto the road. She's silent for a while, chewing on her lip, mulling over what the hell to say to me.

"I'm just frustrated," I finally say, resting my head against the cool glass of the window, "with who she is. How she turned out. It pisses me off that she'd get herself into a place in her life where her son can easily believe some drug dealer killed her."

"What did Marcus say to you?" she asks as she steers the Jeep into the motel parking lot.

After she parks the car, I give her a recap of the conversation I had with Marcus.

"You think he knows where she is?" she asks when I'm finished. She turns off the headlights and the engine.

"I don't know... maybe." I unbuckle the seatbelt and rotate in the seat, looking at her through the darkness flooding the cab. "But it doesn't really matter. What's done is done, I guess."

"You don't mean that." Clara reaches out and brushes my hair out of my eyes. Her touch is soft and affectionate and somewhat calms me down. "You're just upset, which is understandable."

She's right. Deep down I still care about my mother enough to keep searching for her. Time's running out, though, and I'm not sure what I'll do if I don't find her by the time I have to head back home.

"Let's go inside, okay?" Clara drops the car keys into my palm. "We can watch another movie or something. Order pizza."

"What kind of a movie?"

"Whatever kind you want."

"How about a porno? Since you're into those." It takes a lot of energy to make the joke, but I feel better when I do.

She smiles. "And there he is again. I was getting worried about you."

"Worried enough to watch a porno with me?"

"You'd have to be a lot more upset for me to do that."

"Guess I have something to look forward to, then."

Her forehead creases. "What do you mean? I didn't agree to watch one."

"You kind of did, though." I crack the door open, and a breeze gusts into the cab. "I mean, one day, way in our future, I'll be so upset about something you'll have to watch one with me because you said you would."

She rolls her eyes, but doesn't quip back, and I somehow feel like I won her at that moment, like she's agreed to be with me. By the time we get out of the car, I feel so much lighter than I did at the club.

"Thank you for making me feel better," I tell her as we stroll past the motel doors.

"Any time." She glances up at me with compassion in her eyes. "What else can I do to help cheer you up?"

"Well, it is Friday night, so…" I give her a hopeful look.

An uneven breath rushes from her lips then she nods. "Okay."

I can't believe how easily she agreed. "How about, from now on, we just pretend every day is Friday?"

She stares at the ground. "If that's what you want."

I hook a finger underneath her chin and force her to look at me. "It's what I want."

Her eyes flood with so many emotions it's overpowering to watch. I stop and back her up against the wall, needing to kiss her right this instant. I can't wait another second for our lips to connect.

"I like this." With every breath she takes, her chest crashes against mine.

"Like what?" I spread my fingers across on the brick wall behind her, trapping her between my arms.

"This stuff." Her gaze zeroes in on my mouth. "The kissing stuff."

"Good. So do I." My tongue slips out of my mouth, wets my lips as I angle my body over hers.

My eyelids drift shut and I take a deep breath before sealing our lips. She tips her head back, giving me access to kiss deeper as her hands wander down my chest to the bottom of my shirt and sneak up beneath the fabric. My muscles constrict beneath her touch, and my cock instantly goes hard inside my jeans. I'm crossing my fingers that, when we get to the room, she'll let me touch her like I've always wanted to. Skin to skin. Let me all the way in.

Without breaking the kiss, I blindly steer us in the direction of our door, fumbling to get my wallet out so I can retrieve the cardkey.

As I'm feeling around in my pocket, someone clears their throat. I wouldn't think too much of it except that I recognize the smell of the cheap perfume and cigarettes swirling through the air.

I jerk my mouth away from Clara's so abruptly her eyes pop wide.

"W-what's wrong?" she stammers, placing her fingers to her lips.

"It's my—"

"Jax, baby." The skeleton of the woman I used to know cuts me off, strutting toward me with a cigarette between her lips and her arms opened. "Come give Mama a kiss."

Chapter Fifteen

Clara

At the sound and sight of his mother, the color drains from Jax's face. "What the hell are you doing here? I thought you were... dead." His arms fall lifelessly to his sides as he gapes at her in disbelief, as though he's unsure if she's real.

I stare at her in a similar manner, but for a very different reason.

The woman in front of us hardly resembles a person let alone a mother. With boney arms and legs, sunken cheekbones, and saggy skin, she looks too frail to even be standing. Still, if I look at her close enough, I can see the resemblance between her and Jax, at least in the eyes. Although, hers don't convey the same sort of kindness as Jax's.

"Aren't you going to hug me?" She spans her arms to her side.

Jax refuses to budge. "Not until you tell me what's going on."

213

Her gaze is shifty, her body twitchy, like she's either afraid or on something—maybe both. "What, I can't stop by to see my son?"

"Stop by to see your son?" Jas states incredulously. "You're the one who called me saying some guy named Marcus was going to kill you."

She plucks the cigarette from her dry lips, and a cloud of smoke circles her face. "Is that why you came here, to check up on me?"

"I thought you were dead," Jax snaps in the harshest tone I've ever heard him use. "Aunt Julie thinks you're dead, too."

She rolls her eyes melodramatically. "Your Aunt Julie is overdramatic."

"So are you, apparently." He waves his hand in her direction. "Because here you are, clearly fine."

She pops the end of the cigarette into her mouth.

I don't know how, but I have a feeling she's about to say something seriously messed up. Perhaps because of her soulless expression.

"I lied," she divulges as she puffs smoke in Jax's face. "I staged the whole call so you'd come out here looking for me. I knew there was no way in hell you'd come for the real reason. I would have probably tracked you down sooner, but my phone's been disconnected for a while… I wasn't even sure you were here yet, but I ran into Melinda and sure enough, she said my cute little Jax was here looking for me. You were always so good about that."

Rage shockwaves through his body as he lets out a sequence of curse words. Then he spins to the side and bashes his fist into the wall, startling the living daylights out of me. I've never, ever seen him so angry. I just want to hold him and tell him everything will be all right, even though I don't know if it will.

"Jax." I try to soothe him as he punches the wall again and his knuckles split open. "Just calm down."

The anger in his eyes simmers a notch when he sees me staring at him in horror.

I'm sorry, he mouths before he slowly turns to his mother, cradling his injured hand against his chest. "I fucking knew it. I knew there was probably more to that call. Yet, I came here like a sucker."

"You always did care too much," she agrees, flicking the ash from her cigarette. "And trust is your biggest fault." She gives me a look, as if she's warning me to be on the lookout for those traits in Jax, as if being caring and trusting is the worst thing in the world.

"What do you want?" Jax growls before she can say anything else.

She puffs on her cigarette. "A thousand dollars."

A condescending laugh rings from Jax's lips and echoes around us. "Are you being fucking serious right now? Or are you just high?"

Smoke snakes from her lips. "If I don't get it, I'll—"

"Be in trouble with Marcus," Jax finishes hollowly.

"How do you know about Marcus?" She grazes her thumb along the bottom of her cigarette, scattering ashes across the ground.

"We met him while we were looking for you." He flexes his injured fingers. "He said you owe him a thousand dollars and to remind you he isn't a very patient man."

"See, this is why I need your help." She scratches at the back of her neck. "Time is running out."

"I don't get why you think I can help you, though." He shakes his head in annoyance. "I don't have a thousand fucking dollars. I spent everything I did have saved up on this goddamn trip."

"You have no money at all?" she questions, skeptically eyeing him over. "Like zero dollars?

"Nope. I'm flat broke." He seems proud to be telling her this, that he honestly can't give her money. "Guess your little charade was all for nothing."

"Then how are you getting home? I mean, you gotta pay for gas…" She sticks out her hand to him. "Gimme some of that."

Is this woman for real? Seriously, what the hell? My mother, who brought a rooster home, doesn't come off near as crazy as the woman standing in front of me right now.

"I'm paying for the gas," I say, a conniving smile reaching my lips when she directs her attention to me.

Her eyes narrow to slits and places her hands on her hips. "And you are?"

"Jax's girlfriend and the person who's not going to give you the gas money," I explain with sugary sweetness dripping from my voice.

She glares at me. "What gives you the right to speak to me that way?"

I shrug. "I'll speak to you any way I like. I don't know you."

"And yet you judge me," she retorts with disdain.

"It's kind of hard not to when you've made it pretty clear you're the shittiest mother on the planet."

217

She drops the cigarette to the ground and stalks toward me. "You little—"

Jax pushes her, and she trips into the door. "Don't fucking put a hand on her," he warns.

"Don't talk to me like that. I'm your mother," she fumes, her chest heaving with rage as she works to regain her balance.

"Maybe by blood," Jax replies, sounding calmer, "but nothing more."

She opens her mouth to disagree, but then decides against it and snaps her jaw shut. Then she fishes a pack of cigarettes from her pocket and lights up another one. "You really don't have any money?"

I shake my head in astonishment. How can someone like her exist?

"Nope, not a damn dime," he answers, massaging his swelling knuckles.

"Wait a minute..." She notes Jax's injured hand. "You still have that ring I gave you?"

Jax tucks his hand behind his back. "I'm not giving you that back. That's the one damn thing I have that belongs to a family you never let me get to know."

She rolls her eyes, annoyed. "That ring was never your grandfather's. I just told you that to stop you from asking about your father. Seriously, you were such a whiney kid."

"So the story was bullshit?" His confidence weakens. "God, I don't even know why I'm surprised."

She sighs impatiently. "Look, when you were younger, you went through this phase where you kept asking where your dad was after one of your teachers wanted you to make a family tree. Since I don't even have a clue who your father is, I made up a story about your grandfather giving me that ring to give to you one day. It was only to shut you up. I planned on taking the ring back when you were sleeping or something, but I honestly forgot you had it."

"Then whose ring is it?" The hurt in his voice tears my heart apart.

She shrugs indifferently as she stuffs the pack of cigarettes into her pocket. "I have no clue. I jacked it off this rich guy I was screwing. Figured it might be worth something."

The silence that follows is excruciatingly painful.

Shaking his head, Jax yanks off the ring and drops it on the ground. "You know, the really stupid part about this whole thing is that, if you would have just told me over the phone what was going on, I would have sent you the fucking ring."

"I didn't really think about it… I was a little out of it when I called," she explains, scrambling to pick up the ring.

"High as always and your kids are still paying for it." Jax interlaces our fingers, his hand trembling as he swings around and heads for our room. "And FYI, I don't think that ring is worth a thousand dollars." She mutters something unintelligible, and Jax keeps walking, but turns toward her before he unlocks the door to go inside. "Do me a favor, okay?"

"Okay… whatever you need." She barely pays attention to him, focused on the ring in her hand.

"Don't ever fucking call me again." His voice is composed, but his body quivers.

Her fingers curl around the ring. "If that's what you want, then I'll give it to you."

His jaw is set tight as he gives a firm nod. "It's what I want."

"Okay, then." She grins, like she really does believe she's done this great favor for him. Then she hurries away from us and toward the road.

Once she's vanished into the night, Jax releases a deafening exhale as his head slumps against the door. He bangs his forehead against the wood a few times, his body shaking as he takes several erratic breaths. He's crying and I have no clue what to do. I know that, after my father died, I spent a lot of time alone in my room, sobbing my heart out. The loneliness made me feel sad and empty inside, like I'd never feel warm again.

I do the only thing I can think of and wrap my arms around him. "Hey, I know this sounds stupid right now, but it's going to be okay."

"I know it is," he mutters, facing me with his head tucked down. His arms enclose around me and he buries his face in my hair, soundlessly crying.

When he finally pulls away, his eyes are red and puffy. "Sorry." He clears his throat, seeming ashamed by his emotional breakdown.

"Don't apologize. Remember, I'm here for support." I dry a few stray tears from his stubbly cheek with my fingertips. "And look on the bright side. Now you know she's okay, and you can go home."

"*We* can go home," he presses with a smoldering look that makes my skin feel like melting wax. "I really like the sound of that."

"You know what? I do, too," I agree.

With a trace of a smile, he slides the cardkey through the lock and opens the door.

As I'm walking inside the room, I glance back at the desolate parking lot where Jax's mother walked away from her son without so much as a glance back. Even though I've enjoyed my time with Jax, I'm glad to be going home. As stressful as my life is, and as complicated as my mother can make things, I'm lucky I still have her, even if it's just pieces of her.

Chapter Sixteen

Jax

After my mom leaves, Clara and I go into the room and lie down on the bed. My eyes burn from crying and while I should feel like a pussy for being so emotional in front of Clara, I don't.

"I'm so tired." She yawns, stretching her arms above her head.

I roll over beside her, line my body with hers, and drape my arm over her side. Feeling her warmth erases some of the cold my mother put inside me. I forgot how cold I could feel when I am around her. So empty. So un-loved.

"Jax Hensley." Humor laces Clara's tone. "Are you spooning me right now?"

"Yep, it makes me feel better." I nuzzle my face into the crook of her neck and breathe in the scent of her per-fume. "Does that bother you?"

She shakes her head, tipping her chin to look back at me. "If it makes you feel better, then spoon away."

I press closer and place a kiss to her neck right on her pulse.

She shivers, her heart racing. "What do you want to do for the rest of the night?"

As much as I want to peel off her clothes and slip inside her, I don't want to do it while I'm feeling this depressed.

"Can I just hold you while we fall asleep?" I ask, hoping she doesn't run out the door from my request. "I know that seems stupid, but—"

"It's not stupid at all," she interrupts me. Her hands tremble as she places them on my arms and pulls me closer.

I smile against her neck. "I think you might like me a lot, Clara McKiney."

"Maybe."

"Maybe even what? Love me?"

"Shhh…." she whispers, but I can hear the grin through her voice. "Go to sleep."

We spend the rest of the night curled up in bed, spooning each other. It's probably one of the best and worst nights of my entire life. Best, because I have Clara and worst because I realize how much energy I've wasted worrying about my mother all these years.

The next morning I feel a tad bit better. . Not only am I going home, but in the midst of arguing with my mother, I somehow got a bit of closure. For the last couple of years, I've felt so guilty over bailing on my mom when it was clear she couldn't take care of herself, but after that move she pulled to get money from me, my conscious feels clearer.

Now, if I can just convince my sister I'm okay, life will be fantastic.

"Are you sure you're going to be okay driving all the way home?" Avery asks me over the phone. The speaker is on so I can easily chat with her while I pack. "After what happened, I'm a little worried you might be too stressed out."

"I'm fine," I assure her as I stuff a pair of jeans into my duffel bag. "Clara's here with me and she can help me if the stress interferes with my driving skills." I roll my eyes at the absurdity.

"You always say you're fine, even when you're not," Avery argues.

"I'll keep an eye on him," Clara calls out as she walks out of the bathroom wearing shorts that hug her perfect ass, a clinging pink tank top, and towel drying her hair.

"Hey Clara," Avery greets cheerily. "How are you?"

"Fine." Clara drops the towel on the bed then scoops up a brush from the nightstand. "I'm glad to be heading home, though."

"I bet you are," Avery says. I can hear a guy talking in the background, telling Avery to relax. It's probably Tristan, which is good. He's great at getting Avery to chill out when she's in mom mode. "That place can really get to you, huh?"

"The trip hasn't been all that bad." Clara's cheeks flush as she glances at me with a flare of desire in her eyes.

Such a dirty mind, I mouth as I fold a shirt up.

"Good, but just keep an eye on Jax, okay?" Avery says. "He hates admitting when he needs help."

"I will," Clara reassures her while running the brush through her damp hair.

Avery makes me promise her I'll call if I need anything before I hang up.

"She cares about you a lot." Clara stuffs the brush into her bag then winds around the bed toward me.

"She worries too much." I zip up my duffel bag.

"Worrying about someone isn't a bad thing."

"Nope, not at all."

"Are you sure you're okay, though?" she checks, gently grabbing my hand that I bashed into the wall last night. She examines my scraped, swollen knuckles. "Does it hurt?"

I shake my head, watching in fascination as she fusses over me. "Not really."

"What about here?" She lets go of my hand and presses her palm to my chest, right above my heart.

"You're getting soft on me," I joke lightly, even though my heart does ache. "But that's okay. I like this side of you."

Her cheeks pink with embarrassment. "I just want to make sure you're okay."

"I'm fine, so stop worrying." I sweep my finger across her cheek, then pick up my bag and sling it over my shoulder. "Now it's time for me to fuss over you."

She leans over to grab her bag from off the floor, flashing me a great view of her ass. "What do you mean?"

"I mean, it's time to head up to the Tetons."

"I'm going to be fine. It's not like my father just passed away. It's been a couple of years. I've already mourned. This is just for closure and so he can finally be laid to rest."

"I know you've already mourned, but if you get a little bit emotional just know that I'll be right there to hold your hand."

She doesn't say anything, only stands on her tiptoes and places a kiss on my stubbly cheek, which might speak more than words.

"Thank you," she whispers then rushes off to make sure she hasn't left anything in the bathroom.

After we've gathered all our bags and belongings, we head out the door. Then we load up our bags, and check out at the front desk. As we're returning to the Jeep to leave, a sleek, black car pulls up beside us. The tinted windows obscure the view on the interior, but I have a feeling I might know whose inside.

Moments later, the back window rolls down, and my suspicions are confirmed.

I inch to the side, blocking Clara from Marcus's view.

A slow grins curls at his lips. "So, funny thing, your mom showed up last night saying she'd have my money by morning. I woke up thinking I'd be seeing my thousand dollars. Come to find out, she stole a lot of very valuable stuff from me and took off."

There's absolutely no shock factor to what he said. Part of me suspected that my mother more than likely run off with the money she made from the ring instead of paying her debt.

"Okay… What do you want me to do about it?" I ask, glancing around at the parking lot. There's no one around, which isn't an ideal situation. I can see the front desk clerk watching us through the window, which eases my worry just a little.

"Well, I was hoping you could point me in the direction of your mother." He pops a cigarette between his lips and strikes a match, lighting up old school.

"Sorry, but I haven't seen her," I reply coolly as Clara presses her rigid body against my back.

He takes a long drag from the cigarette, the smell of the smoke awakening my nicotine addiction. "That's strange since your mother mentioned she saw you last night."

"My mother's a liar." My voice is firm, despite my nerves being rattled. "You should know that."

He sticks his hand out the window and grazes his thumb across the bottom of the cigarette, scattering ash to the ground. "That I do." He pauses, and I hold my breath, praying he'll leave. "Well, Jax," he sits back in his seat, "it's been a pleasure meeting you. I'm sure one day we'll cross path's again." He starts to roll the window up, but pauses. "And if you do by chance hear from your mother, please let her know I'm looking for her. And remind her how determined of a man I am." He grins one final time. Then the car drives off, kicking up a cloud of dirt behind it.

"Are you okay?" Clara asks, rushing in front of me.

I watch the car pull out onto the street. "You know what, I think I am. Whatever my mother's done, it's no longer my problem. I'm not going to worry about her anymore. I'm sick of getting involved and letting her try to ruin my life."

"Good." She grazes her finger across the inside of my wrist. "She may be your mother, but she's a terrible person and you don't owe her anything.

"I know." I meet her caring gaze and my anger evaporates. "Are you ready to go home?"

She eagerly nods. "More than ready."

Minutes later, we're driving past the final gas station in town. I glance one last time in the rear view mirror, watching my past slip out of sight, knowing it'll be the last time I ever see it.

I'm never coming back, I silently promise myself. *No matter what.*

As difficult as it is to say goodbye, I know it's for the better. I allowed my guilt over leaving my mother gnaw at me for too long.

For the first time in forever, I'm able to breathe freer as I let my past go and head into the future.

The best part is, Clara's at my side.

Chapter Seventeen

Clara

"I think this is about as high as I can go up," I tell Jax, hugging the black vase that carries my father's ashes.

"Are you sure?" He stands on a shallow ledge just above me, staring out at the sparse fields below us with his hands on his hips. He peers up at the pointed, sloped incline of the mountain behind us. "We could go higher if we need to."

I shake my head and remove the lid from the vase. "I can't go higher. I'm already experiencing vertigo."

"Are you afraid of heights?" Jax asks, bounding down onto the small rock I'm standing on.

I nod with a shallow breath. "I actually am."

The wind dances up from behind me and through my hair as I inch toward the ledge. It's cold this high up on the mountains, even in May. I zip my jacket up to my chin while Jax steps back a ways to give me some privacy, which I appreciate.

"Hey, Dad," I whisper as the breeze encompasses me and tears sting at my eyes. "It's me, Clara, your Little Spitfire. I know I've been pretty absent, at last being the spitfire girl you knew, but I'm slowly getting there again, getting happy again. Mom's doing… well, as okay as she can in the condition she's in. I wish I could tell you she's doing great, but I don't think she'll ever be in a place where she's herself again. She does seem pretty happy, though, and Nelli's helping me take care of her." I shrug as I stare at the grassy field below.

"I'm sorry it took me so long to get you up here." I stretch my arms out with the vase grasped in my hand. "I hope you can finally have some peace now." I slowly tip the vase and the ashes float forward with the wind and snow down to the land below. Tears drip from my eyes. "Goodbye, Daddy."

I'm not sure how long I remain standing still, but eventually, Jax moves up beside me.

"Are you going to be all right?" he asks.

I utter one last goodbye then look up at Jax. His hair is sticking up and flattened on one side, and his cheeks are kissed pink from the wind.

"I will be. It's good I did this, good he finally got to be where he wanted to be."

Jax offers me a smile, and then we hike back down the hill to where the Jeep is parked. An hour later we're on the main road again, heading east, heading home.

"Goodbye, Wyoming," I singsong, cranking up "Creep" by Stone Temple Pilots. "I'm not going to miss you at all." I slip my shoes off and relax back in the seat while Jax laughs at my made up song.

"I'm glad to see my hometown made a great impression on you," he remarks, glancing down at the gauges. "I'm with you, though. I'm more than ready to get the hell out of here."

"Are we going to stop anywhere on the way back?" I ask, taking my phone out to text Nelli and tell her my father's ashes have finally been laid to rest.

"Oh, yeah. I have big plans."

"Do I even want to know what those big plans are?"

He slants his head, and hunger gleams in his eyes. "That all depends."

My pulse is throbbing in so many places I can barely sit still. "On what?"

"On how adventurous you feel."

"I'm feeling pretty adventurous."

A sly grin carves his lips. "Okay, then."

His response is so open-ended, so full of possibilities. Surprisingly, I can't wait.

With a lot of effort, I look away from him and focus on texting.

Me: Hey! Just wanted to let you know I'm headed back. I scattered Dad's ashes at the Tetons about an hour ago.

Nelli: How are you doing with that? Are you holding up?

Me: I'm fine. I mean I cried a little, but I don't know... It felt kind of nice to be going through with his final wish, like he can finally be at peace. That probably sounded weird.

Nelli: Not at all. And I'm sure he's at peace.

Me: Can you tell my mom?

She doesn't respond and I figure she's distracted, but then my phone rings, and her name flashes across the screen.

"Hey," I answer. "Thought you'd call me huh?"

"Hey, sweetie." It's my mother's voice that flows through the line, not Nelli's. "I just wanted to call you and say how proud of you I am. I'm sure your father's happy, wherever he is."

She sounds so much like herself I start to cry again.

"I'm sure he is, too," I whisper through my tears.

"I can't wait for you to be home," she says. "We've missed you."

"I've missed you guys, too." I dry the tears with the back of my hand. "A lot."

"Take care, honey." She hangs up.

The conversation is short and sweet, but I'm okay with that. If it had gone on longer, I'm sure she would have faded.

When I set the phone down, Jax slides his arm across the console and threads his fingers through mine. "You good?"

"You know what?" I smile through my tears. "I really am."

We spend the next eight hours holding hands and playing road games. Around midnight, we decide to get a room, even though Jax is still okay with driving. But the stop isn't really about the break.

The moment we step into the room, I stand on my tiptoes and press my lips to his. He reciprocates my kiss, backing me toward the bed until my legs brush against the mattress.

"Are you sure you want to do this?" he asks breathlessly through each swipe of his tongue. "Because we can wait."

Shaking my head, I move back and pull his shirt off. He does the same thing to me, tugging my shirt over my head.

My chest heaves as he deliberately reaches around behind me to unfasten my bra. His eyes remain fastened on me, making sure I don't protest. When my lips stay fused, he unhooks the clasps, and the straps fall from my shoulders.

"You okay?" He sounds a bit hoarse as his gaze consumes every inch of me.

I nod then weld our lips together before I can panic. But it's been so long since anyone has seen me this exposed that I do feel a little jittery. My nerves begin to settle, though, when he presses our bodies together and lays me down on the bed. The warmth of his body drowns out my worry and I fall blindly into kissing him.

We only break apart to finish getting undressed. Once he has a condom on, he situates above me.

"What? No Standing Wheel Barrow this time?" I joke, my jitters revealing through my voice.

Jax shakes his head as he stares down at me. "I'm saving that for another time. Right now, I just want to enjoy this."

He shuts his eyes and sucks in a deep breath before easing into me. He moves torturously slow and I fight back the urge not to lift my hips. By the time he's all the way in me, my skin is already damp.

He starts to rock in and out, our bodies conforming together. He gradually starts to pick up the pace, hitching my leg over his hip, sinking deeper into me. I clutch onto his shoulder blades, my nails splitting his flesh. My skin hums as he drops a kiss on my mouth, parting my lips with his tongue. I bite on his lip and he groans, pounding me hard until I'm so breathless my vision starts to spot. My muscles wind tight, and I start to lose focus as I drift off, grasping onto him.

Seconds later, Jax joins me, burying his face into the crook of my neck. His teeth nick my neck and his body gives one final jerk before he stills, his cock pulsating inside of me.

I swear, in the midst of our heavy breathing, I hear him whisper, "I love you." But he utters it so softly I can't be positive what I heard. What I do notice is that the idea of him saying it doesn't seem too terrifying.

We lie that way for what feels like forever, yet at the same time when he pulls away, I feel as though I could have lain there for so much longer.

He sweeps my damp hair out of my eyes and drops a featherlike kiss on my lips.

"Thank you." He's dead serious and looks very un-Jax like at the moment.

"For what?"

"For letting me in."

My heart misses a beat. "Thank you," I reply back.

"For what?" he wonders.

"For not ruining me when I let you in."

"Never," he promises then leans down to kiss me again. After a minute or two, he pulls away with a crooked smile on his face. "Ready for round two?"

I shake my head, but laugh, feeling more happy and content than I have in a long time.

"Always," I reply and wholeheartedly mean it.

Epilogue

Clara

Three weeks later…

"Oh, my God! Oh, my God! Oh, My God!" I run around the living room like a madwoman because there's a damn mouse scurrying around on the floor.

"Clara, what on earth are you doing?" my mother asks from the recliner.

I squeal like a wimp as I hop onto the coffee table. I have flour on the front of my shirt and cake batter on my hands. Up until a few moments ago, Nelli had been giving me a tutorial on cake baking. Jax's birthday is in less than a month and I need to be prepared to bake the best cake ever.

I'd been doing well, mixing and sifting, while Nelli took a bathroom break. But all of a sudden I was no longer alone in the kitchen.

"There's a mouse…" I search the floor for the little rodent. "Where'd it go?"

My mother gives a noncommittal shrug, and then turns back to the television screen. "He's probably in one of the cupboards again."

My gaze whips in her direction. "What do you mean *again*?"

"I mean, I saw him in there the other day, chewing on a box of crackers."

My gag reflex kicks in and vomit burns at the back of my throat. "Did you throw the box away?"

She shakes her head as she pops a piece of chocolate into her mouth. "Nope."

"Dammit." I mentally psych myself up then jump down from the table and sprint over to the kitchen area. The counters are covered with eggshells, flour, and butter. I pull open all the drawers and open the cupboards, searching for a sign of the mouse. Sure enough, a few boxes of crackers and cereal have been chewed on.

I cringe as I throw each box away into the trash, then I wash my hands and grab my purse from my bedroom. By the time I head back out to the living room, Nelli is back in the kitchen.

"What happened to the cake?" she wonders as she takes in the mess on the counter and stove.

"I ran into a bit of a problem." I drape the handle of my purse over the table. "And now I have to run to the store to get mousetraps."

"We have mice now?" Nelli sits down on the sofa and collects the remote from the armrest as she crosses her legs.

"I guess we have for a while." I give a pressing look at my mother.

My mother shrugs. "It's just a little mouse, Clara. Nothing like a rooster." She smiles at me.

If I didn't know any better, I'd swear she's enjoying my discomfort.

My fingers fold around the doorknob and I crack the door open with my focus still on my mom. "Mice aren't just little; they're gross and disgusting."

"You have mice?"

I jump at the sound of Jax's voice.

"Jesus, you scared me." I press my hand to my racing chest.

"Yeah, I can see that." His brown hair is styled, his grey shirt is just tight enough to show off his solid build, and he's sporting his classic amused grin I've grown to love over the weeks. His grin broadens when he notes the flour on my shirt. "Were you practicing for my birthday?"

"Maybe…" My gaze deliberately scrolls up and down his body before landing on his eyes. I knew he was going to come over this evening to meet my family, which I've been fretting over for weeks. Now that he's here, I'm starting to panic. "What are you doing here? I thought you weren't moving in until later tonight?"

"I got things packed up quicker than I planned." He leans to the side and peers over my shoulder into the living room. "So, you have a mouse?"

"Yeah, it's running around the house." I glance back at my mother who's watching television and then at Nelli who's watching me.

"Are you going to introduce us to your special gentleman friend?" Nelli asks as she unwraps a chocolate bar, staring at us like we're live entertainment. "The one I'm guessing the cake's for."

I shoot her a warning look then turn back to Jax who looks extremely amused.

"Look, *she* thinks I'm a gentleman," he teases with a lopsided grin.

"Yeah, well I'm sure her opinion would change if I told her about all the very ungentleman things you do to me when we're out late."

"Don't pretend you don't like it." His voice drops to a husky whisper. "Besides, I promised you I'd show you those positions, didn't I?"

We exchange a look of desire and my skin erupts with heat. I zip my lips together, unable to deny how much I love being with him.

"Do you want me to see if I can catch it?" he offers. "That is kind of in my job title as boyfriend, right? The guy who gets rid of all the scary things."

"I guess so." I glance back and forth between him and my mother. "Are you sure you're ready to come in… to all of this?"

"Absolutely." He brushes his fingertip across my bottom lip. "Relax. This is a good thing."

I give an unsteady nod. "I know it is."

He moves toward me and drops a kiss on my mouth. "I love you," he whispers in my ear. "So relax."

"I love you too," I whisper to him then step back and let him all the way into my life and heart.

Ruin Me

About the Author

Jessica Sorensen is a *New York Times* and *USA Today* bestselling author that lives in the snowy mountains of Wyoming. When she's not writing, she spends her time reading and hanging out with her family.

Other books by Jessica Sorensen:

The Coincidence Series:

The Coincidence of Callie and Kayden

The Redemption of Callie and Kayden

The Destiny of Violet and Luke

The Probability of Violet and Luke

The Certainty of Violet and Luke

The Resolution of Callie and Kayden

Seth & Grayson (Coming Soon)

The Secret Series:

Ruin Me

The Prelude of Ella and Micha

The Secret of Ella and Micha

The Forever of Ella and Micha

The Temptation of Lila and Ethan

The Ever After of Ella and Micha

Lila and Ethan: Forever and Always

Ella and Micha: Infinitely and Always

The Shattered Promises Series:

Shattered Promises

Fractured Souls

Unbroken

Broken Visions

Scattered Ashes (Coming Soon)

Breaking Nova Series:

Breaking Nova

Saving Quinton

Delilah: The Making of Red

Nova and Quinton: No Regrets

Tristan: Finding Hope

Wreck Me

Ruin Me

The Fallen Star Series (YA):

The Fallen Star

The Underworld

The Vision

The Promise

The Fallen Souls Series (spin off from The Fallen Star):

The Lost Soul

The Evanescence

The Darkness Falls Series:

Darkness Falls

Darkness Breaks

Darkness Fades

The Death Collectors Series (NA and YA):

Ember X and Ember

Cinder X and Cinder

Spark X and Cinder (Coming Soon)

The Sins Series:

Seduction & Temptation

Sins & Secrets

Unbeautiful Series:

Unbeautiful

Untamed (Coming Feb. 2015)

Awakening You (Coming March 2015)

Standalones

The Forgotten Girl

Coming Soon:

Entranced

Steel & Bones

Connect with me online:

jessicasorensen.com

http://www.facebook.com/pages/Jessica-Sorensen/165335743524509

https://twitter.com/#!/jessFallenStar

Ruin Me

18578830R00152

Made in the USA
San Bernardino, CA
19 January 2015